VISION OF THE WITCH
WITCHES OF KEATING HOLLOW, BOOK 10

DEANNA CHASE

Copyright © 2021 by Deanna Chase

Editing: Angie Ramey

Cover image: © Ravven

ISBN: 978-1-953422-03-3

All rights reserved. No part of this publication may be reproduced, stored in, or introduced into a retrieval system, or transmitted in any form, or by any means (electronic, mechanical, photocopying, recording, or otherwise) without the prior written permission of both the copyright owner and the publisher of this book.

This book is a work of fiction. Names, characters, places, and incidents are products of the author's imagination or are used fictitiously. Any resemblance to actual events, locals, business establishments, or persons, living or dead, are entirely coincidental.

Bayou Moon Press, LLC

www.deannachase.com

Printed in the United States of America

ABOUT THIS BOOK

Amelia Holiday never thought she'd be a single mother. But when the father of her child disappears without a trace, that's exactly what she'll be. Moving to the enchanted village of Keating Hollow was supposed to be her fresh start. Only it appears her past has followed her. Now she has to decide if she can trust again or if she's destined to make the same mistakes.

Grayson Riley met the woman of his dreams. The problem? He's a man with secrets and when he had to go back to his old life, he had no choice but to leave her. Now his entire life has blown up, and with the help of his visions, he's looking for a do-over. But will the woman he loves forgive him? Or will he end up losing everything he never knew he wanted?

CHAPTER 1

*A*melia Holiday watched as all the color drained from Grayson Riley's handsome face. That's what happened when one sprung the news on an ex that he was going to be a daddy in five months.

"What—I mean how?" he sputtered, his dark eyes wide and full of panic.

"I think you know how," Amelia said dryly. "You do remember how we spent those few months before you disappeared last December, right?"

"Yes, but…" He shook his head, his forehead creased in confusion. "We used protection."

Amelia snorted out a laugh. "Yeah. We did. Clearly it failed." She slipped past him, ignoring the light roar of the festivities happening all around them. They were at Brian and Shannon's wedding reception at the Pelsh Winery in Keating Hollow, three thousand miles away from the town where they'd last spoken. Every cell in her body was screaming for her to get out of there. To head home and climb into bed under the covers where she didn't have to deal with him. But there was more to say, and if she didn't spit it out right then, she'd only have to tell him later. "But don't worry, Grayson. I don't want or need anything from you. No one is trying to trap you into anything remotely resembling commitment. I just thought you had a right to know. I've got it from here."

Not waiting for a response, Amelia hurried out of the reception hall into the night. The cool February air enveloped her, making it hard to breathe. Or was it more from the reality that she'd just bolted after telling Grayson she was pregnant with his child? She wasn't sure she even wanted to know the answer to that question.

Her heels clattered on the brick walkway as she made a beeline for her car in the large parking lot off to the right.

"Amelia! Wait!" Grayson called from behind her.

Surprise stopped her in her tracks. Although, if she were in her right mind, she would've realized he'd follow her. What decent man wouldn't after the bomb she'd dropped? The problem was that Grayson Riley didn't do relationships. He wasn't the marrying type, and kids were completely out of the question. According to him, his life wasn't built for anything traditional.

Why? She had no idea. She glanced back at the tall man in his expensive-looking wool pants and fitted white button-down shirt. Damn. Why did he have to be so handsome? His charm and good looks were exactly what had gotten her into her current mess. She needed to leave. Now. "There isn't anything to say, Grayson." Amelia gave him a sad smile. "I already know your position on this. There's no need to talk about anything."

He stopped right in front of her and shook his head. "Of course there is. You're pregnant with my child."

She shrugged. "So? I'm having the baby. I'll be raising her here in Keating Hollow. What else is there to say?"

"Her?" he asked with an air of awe.

"Yes," she said quietly. "I just found out a few days ago."

He took a step forward, his gorgeous face alight with wonder as he cupped her cheek with his palm. "You're having our baby. That's... incredible."

Amelia stared at him, her heart racing. All the emotion of the last few months swarmed inside of her, threatening to overwhelm her. This man, the one she'd fallen head-over-heels for, hadn't run the moment he heard the news. How was that possible? Had she gotten everything wrong? Was he pleased by her announcement?

Suddenly, Grayson's expression hardened, and he took a step back, dropping his hand and leaving her cheek cold. "I came looking for you last month. I left my number at the fire station. Why didn't you call me?"

Oh, hell. She knew instantly that she'd messed up. Before, when he'd disappeared without a trace, she'd been the aggrieved party. How was she supposed to tell him about the pregnancy when she hadn't been able to even find him? But he was right. He had left his number at the fire station, and she'd ignored him. She'd told herself she'd get in touch... eventually. If there hadn't been a baby involved, she'd have had every right to ignore him. To never even speak to him again after he pulled his disappearing act. However, this was different. But she'd be damned if she was going to apologize.

After clearing her throat, she crossed her arms over her chest, lifted her chin defiantly, and said, "I was planning to call. I just wasn't ready yet. But I *would have* called."

"It's been two weeks." There was anger in his tight voice.

"Right. And it took you over *two months* to try to find me," she spat out. "*You're* the one who changed your number. You're the one who said you *didn't do love*. What was I supposed to do? Hire a private investigator?"

He winced at her words and glanced away, fixating his gaze on the rows of grape vines that were just visible under the moonlight.

"You know, I did think about hiring a PI," she continued. "But then after cursing you to hell and back, I decided you weren't worth the trouble." That was a lie. But he'd hurt her, and in that moment, all she wanted to do was repay him the favor. "My daughter doesn't need a father who has 'no room in his life for commitments.'" It's what he'd said to her after she'd bared her heart and told him she loved him. His rejection had been immediate, and ten minutes later, he was gone. She spun, intending to stalk off, but he reached out and gently grabbed her wrist.

"Amelia, please."

The pain in his voice stopped her. She glanced back at him. "Please what?"

"Can we go back to my place and talk? It's cold out here and we have things to discuss."

She blinked. "You're living here in Keating Hollow now?"

He nodded.

"Why?"

"I already told you. I'm working for a beverage distributor now. This is my territory."

"Just Keating Hollow?" That couldn't be true. The town wasn't big enough to support its own sales rep.

"No. I have a large portion of the northern California coast. I could've settled anywhere, but Keating Hollow is where…" He paused and ran a hand through his thick dark hair. "Well, when I was here last, I fell in love with it. The people are down-to-earth, and it just felt right."

Amelia narrowed her eyes at him. "Did you make that decision before or after you realized I live here?"

He glanced away again, looking uncomfortable. But then he straightened his spine and stared right at her. Just as he began to open his mouth, she put her hand up, stopping him.

"No. Don't tell me. I don't think I want to know." She sucked in a breath, knowing that he was right. They did need to talk, and she considered his request. She'd prefer to go somewhere public so that she didn't have to be alone with him. But it was getting late, and everywhere she could think of would either be closed due to the wedding or was already booked up due to Valentine's Day. She swallowed a groan. Valentine's Day. Of course.

"Amelia?" The sound of her brother's voice cut through the silence that hung between her and Grayson. "Are you all right?"

"Yes. Of course I am," she said, giving her brother a reassuring smile.

Rex eyed Grayson with suspicion. "Who's this, and what are you doing out here in the cold?"

Amelia sighed. "We were just talking. Grayson Riley, this is Rex Holiday, my brother."

Grayson turned to Rex and held his hand out. "It's nice to finally meet you."

Rex kept his hands in his jacket pockets and eyed Grayson's hand. He raised his gaze and frowned at the other man. "I wish I could say the same."

"I imagine I deserve that." Grayson shoved his hands in his pants pockets and turned to Amelia.

Rex scoffed and opened his mouth to say something else, but Amelia cut him off.

"That's enough, Rex. I can fight my own battles." The last thing she needed was for Rex to insert himself into this mess. He was her protective older brother, and who knew what he'd say to the man who'd broken her heart and knocked her up.

"Fine. But let's get you back inside. It's too cold for you to be standing out here. You don't even have your coat." Rex wrapped an arm around her and tried to steer her back toward the party.

Amelia didn't budge as she shook her head at him. "I'm not going back in there."

"Okay," Rex said, reaching into his pocket and pulling out his phone. "Let me just tell Holly I'm going to run you home and then I'll be right back."

"I don't need—oh. Damn." She'd been so flustered by seeing Grayson again that she'd forgotten she'd come to the wedding with her brother and Holly. Her car was sitting in her garage halfway up the mountain. "You don't need to do that," she said, stopping him from texting Holly. "I'll just go back inside until you're ready to go."

Rex glanced down at her. "You look exhausted. It's not a problem to take you home."

"I'll do it," Grayson said. "We were going to go somewhere and talk anyway."

"No," Rex said, shaking his head. "I've got this handled."

Amelia stared at her brother accusingly. "I can't believe you."

"What?" Rex asked. "I didn't do anything."

She snorted. "You just went all caveman on me. Did you ever stop to think that maybe I can answer for myself?"

Rex blinked at her and then pulled her into a hug and whispered, "Sorry, sis. Are you sure you want to go with him?"

She nodded. "I'm sure. We have to work this out, and it's better we do it now than later."

Tightening his hold on her, he said, "Call me if you need *anything*. And let me know when you're home safe."

Amelia chuckled. "He's not dangerous, you know."

Rex let her go and gave Grayson a skeptical look. "We'll see."

She rolled her eyes. "Go back in before Holly starts to worry. I'm fine."

"If you say so." Rex turned to Grayson. Her brother was a few inches shorter than her ex and had a slimmer build, but his intimidating expression was enough to make Amelia want to take a step back. *Whoa*. Her normally easygoing brother had turned into someone she barely recognized.

"I'll take care of her," Grayson said, appearing unfazed.

"I doubt that." Rex narrowed his eyes at the other man. "But if you hurt her, you'll have me and half this town to answer to."

Grayson nodded. "I would expect no less."

Rex took a step back, his expression turning to one of understanding, and then nodded to Amelia. "See you at your place."

"We're going to Grayson's," she said, just so he wouldn't worry if she wasn't home when they arrived. Rex and Holly lived in Christmas Grove and were staying with her for the weekend.

He frowned at that but didn't say anything as he turned to go back inside.

"Ready?" Grayson asked her.

"Was that some sort of bro code that just went down

between you and my brother?" she asked as he led her to a gray Toyota Highlander.

"It was just a mutual understanding." He opened the passenger door for her.

"What? The one that says you understand that he'll remove your balls with a spoon if you hurt me?" she asked.

He chuckled. "Pretty much." Grayson nodded to the door. "Get in before you get hypothermia."

"It's not that cold," she said as she climbed into the passenger seat.

"Not yet, but it will be." He glanced around at the darkness. "Looks like snow's coming."

"Snow?" She smirked at him, knowing already that the forecast called for a little drizzle and that it wasn't going to get below forty degrees that evening. "Is that wishful thinking or did you just have a vision?"

"I guess we'll just have to wait and find out."

CHAPTER 2

*G*rayson couldn't stop hearing Amelia's words repeat in his mind. *Congratulations, Grayson. You're going to be a daddy in about five months.* That statement had scared the shit out of him. But if he was honest, it also did something to his insides that he couldn't quite explain. There was an ache in his chest that had made him feel both warm and chilled all over.

What exactly was that about? Maybe he was getting a cold. He let out a little scoff and steered his Toyota down Main Street.

"What was that for?" Amelia asked, peering at him from the passenger seat.

He glanced at her, still taken aback by the change in her appearance. He'd always known her as a blonde. But now, her hair was brown and slightly longer than it had been. There'd been no mistaking the curve of her hips or those big brown eyes of hers, though. "I was just… It's nothing."

"Right."

He could almost hear the eyeroll in her tone. And who

could blame her? Grayson was the poster child for keeping secrets. He understood her frustration with him. During the time they'd dated, he'd told her almost nothing about himself. Not anything that was important anyway. It still made him wonder why she'd fallen for him or if she'd only thought she had. How could anyone fall in love with someone who never opened up to them? "Sorry," he said, giving her an apologetic smile. "It really was nothing important. Just me being an idiot."

"Again?" she asked.

Grayson couldn't help it; he laughed. She had every right to call him out on his crap. In fact, it was one of the things that had drawn him to her in the first place. She was strong, self-confident, and definitely didn't need him or any other man in her life to be a success. And even though he knew she didn't need him, he desperately wanted to take care of her. But he'd been down that road before with a woman he'd cared about, and the results had been disastrous. That wasn't a path he could let himself go down again. Not that Amelia would allow it anyway. "It appears to be a pattern."

"I'd say so." She stared out the window at the magical town that was covered in red and pink lights.

Main Street had gone all out for Valentine's Day. The glass globes on the streetlights had been switched to heart-shaped covers; the water in the fountain in the park where they held the farmer's market had been replaced with bubbling pink champagne; each store display had a magical theme; and animated cupids could be spotted periodically, running around shooting their plush arrows at couples strolling down the street. He'd even heard that Incantation Café was selling hot chocolate love potions. Grayson said a silent thanks that he'd managed to avoid that particular concoction. Adding that complication was the last thing he needed.

"It's really something, isn't it?" Grayson said.

"What is?" Amelia turned to him, placing her left hand on her lower stomach.

He wasn't even sure she was aware she'd moved her hand. And god help him, he couldn't deny the tender feelings that rolled through him. "The town. I've never seen anything like it."

"Yeah." She smiled at him, the first genuine smile he'd seen from her that evening. "It's a really special place. My friends say they go all out for every season and holiday. At first it sounded a little overwhelming, but now I love it."

He chuckled. "It felt like walking onto a movie set at first. Over the top, you know?"

She shrugged. "Maybe. But I'd just come from Christmas Grove, the town that oozes Christmas magic all year-round, so it wasn't quite as much of a shock for me."

"Seriously?" He had a hard time imagining living with Christmas year-round.

"Yep. My brother lives there with his girlfriend, Holly. It's a few hours inland from here. It's a lovely place, but I prefer being closer to the coast." Keating Hollow was about thirty miles from the ocean. She narrowed her eyes at him. "If you think it's so over the top, why did you decide to settle here?"

"The people. Also, it didn't take long for the magic of the town to seep into my bones. It just felt… right if that makes sense."

Amelia nodded. "It does. I instantly felt at home here."

After his initial shock, he had too. He'd already accepted the job on the West Coast when he'd found out Amelia had relocated too. At the time, he'd been hopeful they could rekindle what they'd had, though he knew it wouldn't be easy. Not after the way he'd left her last December.

As he turned right into his neighborhood, a light dusting of snow began to fall. He grinned at Amelia. "Told ya."

She squinted at the windshield and shook her head. "You had a vision, didn't you?"

He had, but he didn't want to get into that again, so he just shrugged. "I told you it felt like snow."

"All of the weather reports said low forties." She pulled out her phone and after a few taps, she frowned. "The weather app isn't even updated. It still says chance of rain."

Grayson glanced at the temperature gauge on the dashboard. "It's twenty-nine degrees outside."

Amelia wrapped her arms around herself and gave an involuntary shiver.

That was new. Amelia, a fire witch, was almost never cold. It was why she'd been able to leave the wedding party and not even think about her coat. Grayson reached over and turned the heater up.

"Thanks. My internal regulator has been a little wacky since you knocked me up. Temperature swings aren't unusual these days." She gave him another small smile, and despite the fact that he was freaking out a little at her knocked-up comment, Grayson decided things were looking up.

By the time Grayson pulled into his driveway, the snow had started to stick to the ground. "Come on. Let's go inside. I'll make hot cocoa."

Amelia nodded, climbed out of the Toyota, and followed him into the small, blue, craftsman-style home. "Doesn't Hope Garber from the spa live nearby?"

He nodded "Yep. Right across the street. The house with the red shutters. Why?"

"No reason," Amelia said. "She invited me over one evening for girls' night. I thought the neighborhood looked familiar."

Grayson flipped the light on, illuminating his small living room. It was a little more cramped than he preferred, but it had been the only available rental in town. And it had come furnished, which was a bonus since he'd left all of his furniture behind when he'd left New York a month earlier. Waving toward the leather couch, he said, "Have a seat," before heading straight for the open concept kitchen at the back of the house.

Amelia glanced at it, but instead of taking his direction, she walked over to the kitchen and stood next to him with her arms folded over her stomach. "How can I help?"

"You can grab the chocolate from the pantry." He watched her walk over to the vertical cabinet and admired the long line of her neck. Her skin was so soft, and he'd loved running his thumb over her pulse as it quickened with excitement when he touched her. He'd missed that, those intimate moments, more than he'd realized.

"Stop staring at me like that," she said without turning around.

"Like what?"

"Like you want to strip my clothes off me right here in your kitchen and have your way with me." She grabbed the chocolate and turned toward him with one eyebrow raised.

Grayson chuckled because she was right. He *did* want to do that. It's what he'd hoped would happen before he found out she was pregnant and went into utter shock. Though, if she offered now, he wasn't likely to turn her down. Unfortunately, the look on her face said that wasn't in the cards. At least not anytime soon. "I can't help it if your neck is sexy."

"My neck?" It was her turn to laugh. "It's been a while, hasn't it, Grayson?"

He sobered. "Since early December."

Her eyes widened and she sucked in a breath of air. "I see."

Why had that surprised her? Did she really think he'd left her and jumped right into someone else's bed? *Don't be an idiot, Grayson*, he told himself. What was she supposed to think? He hadn't yet told her anything about why he'd left or why he'd suddenly taken a new job across the country. He cleared his throat and held his hand out for the chocolate. "Hand that over so I can get this going."

She did as he asked and then sat in one of the high-backed chairs at the kitchen island.

He quickly made the hot chocolate, grabbed a plate of cookies he'd picked up from Incantation Café, and then led her into the living room.

Amelia curled up under a blanket in the corner of his leather couch.

Grayson knew he should probably take the matching chair, but he just didn't want to be that far away from her. Instead, he sat at the other end of the couch, eyeing the blanket.

"Don't even think about it," she said, tightening her hold on the throw. "Get your own."

He laughed. "That one is mine."

"Not anymore." She smirked at him and took a sip of her hot chocolate. The look of pure pleasure on her face, combined with her moan of appreciation, made him have to stifle a groan. "It's really good," she said. "Like award-worthy good."

"I think it's just been a long time since you've had hot chocolate," he said, but he felt a rush of warmth run through him due to her compliment.

"I had it two days ago. It wasn't anything like this. What did you put in it? Some sort of spice?"

"There's a couple actually. Haven't you ever had Mexican hot chocolate?" he asked her.

She shook her head and took another sip, closing her eyes as she savored the drink. "This is truly incredible."

"You're incredible," he said and immediately regretted it. What the hell was he doing? That wasn't something he should be blurting out. They had a lot more important things to talk about other than how much she dazzled him.

Amelia lowered the mug and frowned at him. "That can't be true."

"Yes, it can," he said firmly, apparently going all in on his stupidity. "You're the most incredible woman I've ever met."

She scoffed and got to her feet. "Don't do that."

"Do what?" He stood, taking a step so that they were just inches apart. "Tell you the truth?"

"Say things like that after what happened back in Cape Cod. It's... cruel." They'd been spending the week in Cape Cod when Grayson got the call. He hadn't even waited until they got back to New York before leaving her.

Amelia walked away from him and headed to the kitchen where she put her mug in the sink. "I think you should just take me home. It's obvious we aren't going to talk about the elephant in the room, and I could really use some sleep."

Grayson walked slowly over to where she stood in his kitchen. "I'm sorry. I shouldn't have said that."

"No. You shouldn't have. You made yourself perfectly clear a few months ago when you said you weren't a relationship guy, and I heard you. I wouldn't have come here with you if it weren't for this little one I'm carrying around." She pressed both hands to her belly, appearing protective of their child. "Flirting just makes everything harder."

Dammit. He'd known he was messing this up the minute he'd uttered the words. "Listen, Amelia, I'm sorry. You're right, I—"

She held her hand up, stopping him. "No need to apologize. Let's just drop it, okay?"

He nodded, eager to move on. He felt too much like an ass already. During that same Cape Cod trip, right after he'd gotten that call, she'd told him she loved him. And what had he said? *I like you, too.* That statement had been followed up with a big 'but,' and he'd quickly laid out all the reasons why he couldn't be in a relationship. He'd broken her heart. That hadn't been hard to figure out, but what she didn't know was that his had broken, too. He'd wanted to tell her how he felt, actually *ached* to tell her, but his life had been too complicated.

Shaking his head to clear his thoughts, he said, "There are a few things I need to tell you before I take you home."

"What's that?" she asked, sounding suspicious, like she was waiting for him to drop another bomb.

He sucked in a deep breath and let it out slowly. "Let's go into the living room and sit down while we talk."

Amelia nodded and followed him. They sat on opposite ends of the couch and turned to face each other.

Grayson tapped his fingers on his knee, trying to ignore the fact that his nerves were on edge. "I'm not going to pretend that your news hasn't rocked me. It most definitely has."

"I figured," she said, slumping back against the arm of the couch and closing her eyes as if she wanted to hide her pain from him.

His heart hammered in his chest, and he longed to take her in his arms, but he knew he couldn't. Not now. He had no right to touch her like that anymore. "I'm a lot of things, some good, some not great, but one thing that I am is loyal. When you told me that you didn't expect anything from me, that you'd raise our daughter on your own, that gutted me."

Her eyes flew open and flashed with fire. "What was I

VISION OF THE WITCH

supposed to say? I know you don't do commitment, but here we are. Get used to it?"

Most people Grayson knew *would* say that. It didn't surprise him that it hadn't occurred to Amelia to take that same path. She was far too independent and proud to expect anything from someone who didn't want to be in her life. But she had no idea just how much he wanted to be there with her. And their child. "You could have. You had every right to. But that's beside the point." He couldn't help himself. Reaching out, he slipped his fingers through hers and squeezed. He needed to touch her, to be connected with her somehow. "I'm not going to let you do this without me. I'll be here, every step of the way."

Grayson meant every word, but there was a hollow feeling in his stomach. His life hadn't really been his own for over a decade. Between the time he'd left Amelia and landed in Keating Hollow, he'd finally cut ties with his past commitments. But could he stick with his decision? If Kira called, would he ignore her? He hoped like hell he would because there was nothing he wanted more than a family. And he knew better than most how toxic Kira's life could be. He just didn't know if he could live with himself if he ignored her call and something terrible happened like it had a few years ago.

"I don't know what to say to that," Amelia said, staring at their hands that were still connected.

"You don't need to say anything. I just needed you to know that's where I'm at with this."

"You just found out less than an hour ago." She pulled her hand from his and clasped both of hers together. "I don't think now is the time for declarations."

"No?" he asked, trying to keep the defensiveness from his

voice. "What about you? How did you feel when you first found out you were pregnant?"

"Scared and pissed off."

He almost chuckled at the irritation on her face. "Okay. Understandable. But what about after that? Did you consider walking away from her?"

Amelia jerked her head back in shock, her eyes going wide again. "Of course not. I'd never do that."

He smiled gently at her. "That's exactly how I feel."

Amelia stared at him for a long moment before she finally nodded. "Okay. Fair enough. What's the second thing you need to tell me?"

This was harder. There were things he couldn't tell her, though he wanted to. Damn, did he want to. "There are parts of my life that I can't talk about."

She snorted. "No kidding. I got that when you disappeared the last time. What are you, a spy or something?"

If only it were that simple. And he couldn't blame her for thinking that. Less than twenty-four hours after he'd left her in Cape Cod, his phone had been replaced and all of his things from his rental in New York had been packed up and sent to storage. He cocked his head and met her gaze. "Do I look like a spy?"

"No." She raked her gaze over him. "You look like a businessman who travels extensively and picks up a lot of women in hotel bars."

Chuckling, he shook his head. "You're the only woman I've ever picked up in a hotel bar."

Amelia rolled her eyes. "Sure, Grayson."

He hated that she didn't trust him. It was his own fault though. "I'm not a spy. But you should know that the reason I left you was because I had responsibilities that I couldn't ignore. A call came in and I had to go."

"That sounds like you're either a spy or an agent with the witness protection program," she said.

"I imagine both of those would be easier to explain," he said with a sigh. "Let's just say this was... a family obligation."

Her entire body tensed as she gritted her teeth and asked, "You're not married already, are you? Because if I was sleeping with a married man, I swear on everything that is holy that I will find a way to hurt you, Grayson Riley."

He held his hands up in a surrender motion, shaking his head. "I swear I'm not married. No other kids. It's not like that. I promise."

The tension drained from her face, and she looked at him curiously. "You're saying you left so suddenly because of a family obligation?"

"Yes, something like that." Feeling completely exposed, he averted his gaze. He didn't want to be talking about this, but he had to give her as much of the truth as possible. "Someone I cared for needed me, and I went to help pick up the pieces of their life after everything went to shit. It's not the first time, not even close. But it's the last. We've parted ways. For good."

Amelia eyed him suspiciously. "An ex?"

"Sort of. We dated for a short while a long time ago. I can't really talk about it. I'm sorry. I would if I could."

Amelia waved a hand, indicating that his confession wasn't that big of a deal. "You don't need to explain it to me. You don't owe me anything."

That's where she was wrong. He owed her everything.

CHAPTER 3

Amelia didn't know how she felt about Grayson's confession. So he had a past he couldn't talk about. One that wasn't resolved while they were together. She wasn't sure she believed him when he'd indicated that the person wasn't an ex. Obviously, whoever it was had been important enough for him to run when they called. Still, he'd completely changed his life in the past month, hadn't he? And he hadn't run when she'd announced she was pregnant. Those were good signs.

Trust was hard to come by though, especially considering her own past, and at that moment, all she really wanted to do was go home and unwind. Let herself process the day's events. Grayson was living in her town and wanted to be a part of her and her child's life. That was good, right?

Honestly, it was overwhelming.

"Are you okay?" he asked, concern radiating off him.

"Yeah. Just wiped out. Do you think you could take me home now? It's been a long day, and I get tired easily now."

"Of course." There was disappointment in his handsome expression, almost making her laugh.

When they'd reconnected at the wedding, it'd been obvious he'd wanted to start right back up where they'd left off. If things had been different, she might have been right there with him. Because there was no denying the chemistry that sparked between them. Even now there was a pull drawing her toward him. How easy it would be to fall into bed with him again and forget for a while all that had happened in the past few months.

Too bad she was still working with a rational brain. Sex couldn't be on the table. Not now. The stakes were too high. They had a daughter to think about. Besides, what if he decided to bolt after he had time to think things over? Her heart wouldn't survive it. "Let me just use the restroom before we go."

"It's down at the end of the hall." He waved to the narrow hallway sandwiched between the living room and kitchen area.

Amelia hurried down the hall, focused on the business at hand. When she emerged, she couldn't help but notice the flash of red in the bedroom to the left and did a doubletake. Stopping in her tracks, she stared at the red rose petals scattered on the gray bedspread. There was also a collection of candles set up on the dresser but not lit. She blinked. He really had been expecting to seduce someone.

The sound of Grayson clearing his throat behind her made her jump and press a hand to her heart.

"Seriously?" she said as she turned around to face him. "You were expecting me to fall into bed with you?"

He gave her a sheepish smile. "It's rare when my visions don't come true. But maybe I jinxed it when I added the rose petals. I didn't exactly see that part. But it's Valentine's Day, so... I went all out."

"What did you see?" she asked, raising one eyebrow and immediately regretting it when he stared down at her with a sexy half-smile.

"You, naked, leading me to the bed."

Her mouth went dry as she glanced at the rose petals again, and she knew if she didn't get out of there right then she was likely to make his vision a reality. There was just a chemistry with Grayson that she couldn't deny. Goddess help her, she didn't even want to. Brushing past him she said, "It's time to go."

He let out a quiet sigh from behind her as he followed, his footsteps echoing on the wood floors.

Before they reached the door, Grayson grabbed a coat off of his coat rack and handed it to her. "Here. Put this on."

She glanced at the long wool coat and almost declined it, but when she looked out the window, the snow had really started to fall. Even with her ability to usually stay warm despite the elements, she had to be responsible. It wasn't just her she had to take care of anymore. "Thanks."

He nodded, pulled on a jacket, and held the door open for her.

Amelia hurried out into the snow, the chill stinging her face. Holy hell. It almost never got that cold in Keating Hollow.

Grayson held the door open for her and then jogged over and jumped into the driver's side. He started the vehicle and rubbed his hands together, warming them up. "Good thing we're leaving now. It looks like it's going to get thick out here tonight."

Amelia nodded, hoping that her brother and Holly were already on their way home.

Grayson pulled out of his driveway, but before he took off down the street, he pumped the breaks and stopped next to a black truck. The hood was open, and two young men were peering at the engine.

Grayson lowered his window. "Hey guys. Everything okay here?"

The taller one turned to Grayson, and Amelia instantly recognized him as Silas Ansell, a young Hollywood star and the brother of newlywed Shannon Ansell-Knox, who'd taken up residence in Keating Hollow when he was between jobs. The slightly shorter, curly haired teen beside him was his boyfriend, Levi Kelley, Hope Garber's brother. Silas shook his head. "Levi's truck won't start. We'd just stay here at his house, but I have a new puppy at home who needs dinner."

"Hop in," Grayson said without hesitation. "I'll give you a ride."

"Are you sure?" Silas asked. "My house is halfway up the mountain."

"You're in luck. Because Grayson is headed that way. I think we might be neighbors," Amelia said, remembering that she'd heard the gorgeous house that had recently been built behind hers belonged to the star. "I rent the Bradley place."

"Perfect." He glanced at Levi. "That okay? It means you might be stuck at my place for the night."

Levi laughed. "That's not a hardship." He grinned at his boyfriend and the pair hurried to climb into Grayson's Toyota.

"Hi, I'm Silas," he said to Amelia. "I'm not sure if we've met."

She glanced back at him. "Not officially." She offered him her hand. "Nice to meet you. I'm Amelia Holiday."

"Glad to finally meet my neighbor. I apologize for not coming around, but…" He shrugged. "I can be a recluse when I'm in town."

Levi snorted. "He's not really that anti-social. It's just hard to know how people are going to react when they meet *the* Silas Ansell."

Silas cast him a dirty look. "You don't have to throw me under the bus. What if she didn't know who I was? You ruined my chances of anonymity."

Amelia laughed. "Too late. I already knew. But don't worry. I won't be peeking in your windows or going through your trash." She winked at him. "Not yet anyway."

He let out a humorless laugh. "If only you knew how often that happens."

"It does? Here in Keating Hollow? You can't be serious."

"Oh, no. Not here. It happens mostly when I'm in LA." He gave her a small smile. "The witches in this town don't put up with that kind of nonsense. And then there's Levi." He gave his boyfriend a tender glance. "One of his gifts is sensing people. That makes it harder to spy on us."

"That's a handy skill." Amelia smiled at them, loving the way they were looking at each other. Love radiated off them, making her heart swell.

"It is." Silas reached over and took Levi's hand in his, and Amelia turned around, feeling like she was a third wheel in that moment.

"So, Amelia, how do you know Grayson?" Levi asked a few minutes later.

Amelia opened her mouth to answer but then closed it, not knowing what to say. That they'd dated? That he was the father of her baby? Both felt entirely too personal to just blurt out to the neighbors.

"Amelia and I knew each other in New York. It was a surprise to both of us that we both ended up here," Grayson said easily as he made the turn up the winding mountain road that led to her rental.

"Really? That's cool," Silas said. "And you're both here for good now?"

"That's the plan," Amelia said. "I work at the fire station. Fire witch."

"Sweet. Now I know what to do when I can't get the fire started in my wood stove," he said.

She chuckled. "Happy to help."

They chatted about the movie Silas had just wrapped and what jobs he had coming up. Levi was quiet for most of the conversation, only speaking when they turned into Amelia's driveway and got a look at the modern three-bedroom that she'd been lucky enough to rent after the Bradley's moved Back East due to a new job opportunity. "This is a really cute house, Amelia. I bet it's easier to keep clean than the monster Silas built."

"My house isn't a monster. It's only four bedrooms," Silas insisted.

Levi snorted. "Four bedrooms and an office all for one person."

"When I'm here, there's usually two of us. And now I have a dog, too," Silas said indignantly. "And there's room to grow. What if we… er, I have kids some day?"

"Kids?" Levi asked, his voice shaky and full of both surprise and terror.

"One day. Maybe." Silas slipped his fingers through Levi's and then kissed the back of his boyfriend's hand. "It was just a thought for some time in the future."

Levi was shaking his head when they all heard a loud crack followed by a thundering boom.

Amelia jumped about a foot and her heart pounded as she

stared at the tree that had just fallen across the road about twenty feet from her driveway. "Holy hell," she muttered, clutching her chest. "That was way too close."

Grayson wrapped his arms around her, pulling her into him while Silas and Levi clung to each other. "We better get everyone inside. The snow is coming down wetter and heavier than I anticipated." He glanced at Amelia's house. "Whoever built here did a good job of clearing around the house. It's unlikely any trees will fall on it."

The four of them hurried to the house, and Amelia quickly let them all in. They stood at the front window, watching as more and more snow accumulated on the mountain. "It looks like you're staying here," Amelia said to Grayson. "Your Toyota is blocked for the time being."

He shrugged, clearly not at all bothered by the news.

"We should get to my house before it gets worse, "Silas said. "It won't be too far if we cut through the tree line at the edge of the property."

"Be careful," Amelia said, eyeing the snow. "Stick together and if visibility is bad, come right back here. I have an extra guest room you can use. It's the nursery, but there's a double bed in there, too. Holly and Rex are using the other one."

"Thanks, Amelia. I think if we go now it won't be too terrible." Silas squeezed her hand and then turned to Grayson. "Thanks again for the ride." The two teenagers waved as they headed toward her back door.

"We'll be here if you need anything," Amelia called after them.

"Thanks," Levi replied as he followed Silas out into the snow.

Amelia watched until she saw them disappear into the thin tree line between their two houses.

Grayson turned to her. "Looks like it's just us."

It was then she realized that her brother and Holly hadn't made it home yet. She grabbed her phone and sent a quick text. A moment later, Rex texted back that they were still in town and conditions were worsening. It looked like they were going to stay at the inn for the night. "It really is just us," she said to Grayson, her heart speeding up at the prospect of the two of them alone in the house for the night. She quickly turned away and went to her wood burning stove. "I'll get the fire going."

"Are you hungry?" he asked. "I don't mind making something if—"

"I'm fine," she said, waving a dismissive hand. "I had enough to eat at the reception. If you want something, feel free to take a look and see what you can find."

Grayson nodded and disappeared into the kitchen that was to the left of the living room.

After changing out of her dress and into something more comfortable, Amelia walked out onto her back deck, collected a bundle of firewood from her storage shed, and returned to the living room where she used her magic to start the fire in her wood stove. Before long, the heat warmed the small modern house as she curled up with a blanket on the couch and stared out the front window at the stunning view of snow covering the Keating Hollow valley. In the distance, she could just make out the river that ran through town, and she wondered, not for the first time, how she'd gotten so lucky to find such a magical place.

"This is a truly gorgeous location, Amelia," Grayson said from behind her.

She glanced back at him, finding him rocking on his heels as he too stared out her picture window.

"Sometimes I can't even believe that I'm here."

"I'll forever picture you like this from now on." He dropped his hands onto her shoulders and gently massaged.

"Damn, that feels good," she said, closing her eyes and reveling in his touch. He knew exactly how much she loved being massaged, and while she knew she should ask him to stop, it just felt too good.

He dug his thumbs into the muscles at the base of her neck and said, "I have a surprise for you."

"What surprise?" she asked, not really caring about the answer.

"You have to get up to see it."

She glanced back at him, narrowing her eyes in suspicion. "What are you up to?"

He rounded the couch and held his hand out to her. "Come on. You're going to want this."

Her defenses were down, and she was suddenly too relaxed to resist him. She slipped her hand into his and let him help her off of the couch.

He put one hand on the small of her back and gently guided her down the hall.

Amelia eyed him. "What are you up to? I'm not sleeping with you." She said the words automatically, but there wasn't any heat behind them.

Grayson just chuckled. "So I've already been told." He tugged her into her master bedroom, but instead of stopping near the bed like she expected him to, he continued to guide her toward the master bath. After pushing the door open, he nudged her in. "Back at Shannon's wedding, you did tell me you had a vision of relaxing in the tub instead of spending the night with me. As pained as that makes me," he said with a smirk, "I didn't want your vision to be ruined just because I'm here, so I got your bath ready for you."

"You did this?" she asked as she stared at the cup of tea and lit candles on the ledge of the tub around the bubble bath that had been drawn.

"Well, it wasn't Silas or Levi." He winked and then backed out of the room. "Enjoy it. I'm going to make myself at home in the guest room."

"Grayson?" she said before he closed the door.

"Yeah?"

"Thanks for this."

"You're welcome."

When he was gone, she got undressed and slipped into the warm water with a contented smile on her face. There was a reason she'd fallen in love with him back in New York.

CHAPTER 4

*G*rayson woke early. He'd lain awake half the night thinking of Amelia in the other room, wishing he was with her and holding her close as she slept. He'd missed her more than he'd realized. Just being near her calmed him, quieted all the voices in his head that questioned his life choices. He wasn't on edge or worried about what came next. He was just happy to be in the moment.

It was the complete opposite of being in Kira's presence.

He knew now that he'd been crazy to let Amelia go back in December. But he'd spent years making tabloid stories go away about Kira, and that was a hard habit to break. Especially since she'd been the one person who'd been there for him when he'd needed someone the most.

Things were different now. They had been for a few years, but he hadn't been able to see it. It wasn't until he got back to New York City and found Kira knee-deep in another round of self-destruction that he'd done what he could to put her back together and then told her he was done for good.

That hadn't gone over well, but by the time he'd left, he felt certain that he was finally moving on. He had given everything of himself that he'd had to give, and the star would just have to figure out how to navigate her life without him.

Grayson peered out the window to find the snow was still coming down. It was clear he wasn't going anywhere anytime soon. He padded into the kitchen, wearing his clothes from the day before, and made a pot of coffee. Then he got to work making breakfast.

Just as he was setting the table, he heard Amelia's footsteps in the hall. He glanced back and spotted her in her flannel pajamas and a thick robe. Smiling at her, he said, "Good morning."

"Morning." She glanced at the waffles, bacon, and fresh fruit and then stared at him in surprise. "You did all this?"

"It appears so." He handed her a mug of coffee, doctored with her favorite vanilla creamer. "Have a seat."

She slipped into one of the chairs at her table and smiled up at him. "I could get used to this."

Warmth spread through his chest, and he gave her a quiet smile as he said, "So could I."

Amelia's cheeks turned pink, and she suddenly became very interested in her waffle.

Grayson sat beside her and watched her for a moment before he filled his own plate. Silence built between them until finally he said, "I'm going to miss this when the snow clears."

She lifted her head, caught his eye, and smirked. "You mean making me breakfast and waiting on me hand and foot? I'm going to miss that, too."

He chuckled. "If there's an opening for that position, I'll gladly throw my hat in the ring."

Grinning, she said, "You're hired."

"Offer accepted. Now you're never getting rid of me." His

tone was teasing, but he meant every word. He'd already decided that if she'd give him another chance, he was going to show her that he was all in.

Her grin faded as his words seemed to sink in, but Grayson pretended he didn't notice. She'd see soon enough. After they were done with breakfast, Grayson cleared the table and asked, "Do you have a chainsaw?"

"What?" she asked, clearly taken aback by his question.

"A chainsaw. If you have one, I can work on removing the tree from the road so that when the snow removal service gets up and running your road can be cleared."

She frowned. "I have no idea. We can check in the shed."

"Okay, I'll do that after I finish these dishes."

Amelia stared at him as he started to load the dishwasher. Then she shook her head. "What are you doing?"

"The dishes?"

She rolled her eyes. "You know what I mean. First the bubble bath, then breakfast, and now the dishes. You want something. What is it?"

Grayson placed the plate in his hand in the dishwasher and turned around, leaning against the counter as he decided to be completely honest with her. "You."

Amelia blew out a breath. "Grayson, you walked away from me. Remember?"

"I did, and I regret it every day."

She crossed her arms over her chest and stared at him, her brows pinched and distrust in her big dark eyes.

The look on her face felt like a gut punch. He knew he deserved her reaction, but that didn't mean it didn't kill him. "I know it's too soon to be having this conversation. That I need to earn your trust. But I thought I'd just make myself perfectly clear. I didn't walk away from you because I didn't want you. I did it because I felt I had to. My circumstances have changed, and if you'll let me, I'll do anything I can to prove to you that you can trust me."

"It's not going to happen in less than twenty-four hours," she said, her tone chilly.

Damn. She wasn't giving an inch, was she? That was okay. He wasn't going anywhere. "I know. Just making sure you know my intentions." He winked at her and went back to finishing the dishes. After a moment, he heard her let out a huff and then retreat back to her bedroom.

Grayson finished up the dishes, and just as he was getting ready to go look for a chainsaw, his vision turned dark. When it cleared, he was standing in an unfamiliar room, overlooking a dramatic coastline. The furniture was all white, the walls void of any color. He stood in the middle of the room, staring down at Kira, who was draped over a chaise lounge wearing nothing but a short silk robe. She held her hand out to him and said, "Welcome home, Grayson."

His vision turned dark again, and when he blinked, he was back in Amelia's blue-gray kitchen. He grabbed the counter and sucked in a sharp breath, his heart racing with trepidation.

"No," he whispered under his breath with intense conviction.

That wasn't happening. It was rare that his visions didn't come true. It had only happened a few times in his life. But if there was one thing he knew for sure, it was that under no circumstance would he let this one come to pass. When Kira called, and he knew she would, he would not be answering. He'd been back in Amelia's life for less than twenty-four hours, and he already knew he'd do anything to stay with her.

He was one hundred percent done with sacrificing himself for someone who only cared about herself.

CHAPTER 5

*A*melia stood in the shower, letting the hot water beat on her neck. After her bath the night before, she'd curled up in her bed and slept more soundly than she had in weeks. Finally, Grayson knew that he was going to be a father, and to her utter surprise, he hadn't run.

She hadn't realized just how much stress she'd been under because of the fact that he didn't know. And she was intensely relieved that he hadn't hated her for not getting in touch right after he'd first shown up in town a few weeks earlier. She'd been a coward. There was no disputing that. It was just that she'd been so hurt when he left back in December. It wasn't something she wanted to go through again.

That was why it was so hard to hear Grayson say he wanted her. The pain she'd been through the last couple of months had been unbearable. If he walked out again, she wouldn't be able to survive it. The pain of baring her soul and having him reject her was still too fresh. Even though he was declaring he was back in her life for good, it wasn't as if he'd told her he loved her. He hadn't promised anything. For all she knew, he'd only had a change of heart because Amelia was pregnant with his child. She was willing to let him back into her life, but the door was closed when it came to her heart. It wasn't a risk she was willing to take.

After her shower, she took her time drying her hair and making herself look presentable. When she finally emerged, she was wearing jeans, a T-shirt under a thick sweater, and wool socks, and she was ready to curl up by the wood stove. But when she saw that Grayson had indeed found a chainsaw and was out in the snow cutting up the fallen tree, she sighed, changed into an old sweatshirt, tugged her boots on, and trudged out into the wintery weather to see if she could help.

"Hey, gorgeous," he said, smiling at her. He'd changed into a pair of sweats and a sweatshirt.

"Where'd the outfit come from?" she asked.

"My Toyota. Gym bag." The chainsaw was laying off to the side of the road, and it didn't take long for her to figure out that he'd already cut up the tree and all that was left to do was to move the pieces of the trunk off the road. He studied her. "Whatcha doing out here?"

"I came to help." She reached down for a piece of the trunk.

"No, don't do that. I've got it," he said, already moving toward her, clearly intending to stop her from lifting anything.

But it was too late. She'd already reached for a cut piece of the log. But as soon as she tried to pick it up, she felt a twinge in her back and stopped immediately. "Oh, ouch! That hurts."

Grayson closed the distance in seconds and placed his hands on her hips from behind, stabilizing her. "Where does it hurt?"

"My lower back. Guess I should've bent my knees, huh?"

"You shouldn't have been lifting it at all. For the goddess's sake, Amelia, you're pregnant." He didn't sound mad. He sounded worried. "Come on. Let's get you back inside."

"I'm all right," she said, slowly trying to stand upright again. But the pain in her back made her wince. "Oh, damn. That's not good."

"Come on. Grab my arm. I'll help you back up to the house."

She did as he said, and slowly she inched through the snow. By the time they made it back to her front steps, her teeth were chattering from the cold and her lower back had completely seized up. "I desperately need a healer."

"Let's just get you inside and then we'll figure out what to do from here."

It was only with his help that she was able to navigate the steps onto the porch, and once she was back in her house, she immediately crawled onto her floor, lying flat on her back as she just breathed through the pain. "This isn't good," she said through clenched teeth. "I don't think a healer is going to be able to get up here."

"I'll call the healers in town and see if they have any advice," Grayson said, already reaching for his phone in his back pocket.

Amelia stared at the open beam ceiling and listened as Grayson spoke to Gerry Whipple. When he said that she was pregnant, Amelia covered her abdomen with both hands and cursed herself for not being more careful. She knew that some physical activity was fine at this stage in her pregnancy, but now that she was hurt, she didn't exactly care what the experts said. All she wanted was to be healthy for her child.

Grayson listened to the healer and then asked Amelia, "Do you have any emergency pain potions or herbs to make one?"

"I don't want to take anything that will harm the baby," she said automatically.

"I know. She said there are a few things you can try that are safe."

"It doesn't matter anyway," she said through clenched teeth. "I tossed the potions last month. As for herbs, you'll have to check. I know I have dill and chives, but I doubt those work for pain."

"I'll see what you have." He disappeared into her kitchen. A few minutes later, he emerged with a grim look on his face. "The only thing you have is some ginger, but it would be better if you had some green tea to go with it."

"No green tea," she said with a hiss. "I'm a coffee girl."

"I noticed. I'm going to make a ginger and honey concoction. It's the best we can do for now. But I'll get some ice for you first."

Amelia groaned but knew he was right. Maybe she should've just stayed out in the snow.

A knock sounded on the door. Instinctively, Amelia tried to push herself up but immediately abandoned that idea when a bolt of pain shot down her leg. "Son of a cupid's butt," she muttered.

The door cracked open, and Levi poked his head in. "Amelia, I'm so sorry, but I saw you lying there on the floor through the window. Are you all right?"

"Hey, Levi. No need to apologize. I wasn't going to be able to make it to the door. Come on in."

The teenager slipped inside with Silas and a fuzzy yellow puppy right behind him.

"I hope you don't mind. We brought Cappy with us. Didn't want him to get cold," Silas said.

"Not at all," Amelia said, dying inside because she couldn't scoop the adorable thing up into her arms. "He's precious."

"Thanks." Silas gave her a grateful smile as they stripped themselves of their boots and jackets. When he was done, Levi moved to sit right down on the floor next to her, while Silas held the puppy back so he wouldn't jump all over her. "What happened?" he asked.

"I threw my back out. Grayson is making me some ginger concoction since we can't get out to see a healer. What brings you two by?"

Silas, who'd taken up residence on her couch with the puppy at his feet, leaned forward and said, "Power's out at Chez Ansell. We wanted to check and see how things were going here." He glanced around. "Looks like we're the only unlucky ones."

Amelia said, "Let's hope it lasts. Any idea what knocked yours out?"

"We didn't see any lines down."

"You're welcome to stay here until you can get down the mountain or the power is restored," Amelia said. "I have plenty of food, and I'm pretty sure there's a whole home generator if we lose power."

"Mine's not being installed until next month," Silas said with a sigh. "The unit we ordered was backordered. Thanks. I appreciate it."

"No problem." She smiled at the actor and then turned her attention to Levi. "What are you doing here on the floor with me?"

"If you're up for it, I think I can help," he said, gesturing to her back. "I've been working with Healer Snow over in Eureka."

"Um…" She bit her lower lip, unsure what to do. The pain

was dreadful, but she didn't want to do anything that would risk her child.

"What is it?" he asked, his brows knit.

"Nothing, I..." Amelia blew out a breath. "I'm pregnant, and I just don't want to do anything that could be harmful."

Levi broke out into a grin. "That explains the conflicting energy I feel coming from you. I gotta say, that was really strange, but your pregnancy makes perfect sense."

"You can feel my energy?" she asked. "Spirit witch?"

He nodded. "Your daughter is a strong one, too. I don't think you need to be worried. I can help your back without affecting her in anyway."

"You knew she was a girl?" Amelia asked, astonished. "How?"

"I can just tell." He scanned her body. "If you lie on your side, I think I can help."

"It should be okay," Grayson said from across the room. He was holding a mug that had steam curling from inside. "Gerry Whipple said a healer would be able to ease the tension with their touch."

Levi nodded. "That's exactly what I plan to do."

Amelia sucked in a deep breath and winced when the pain shot down her leg again. That was all she needed to get her to roll over. "Go ahead. I can't spend the rest of my life here on the floor."

"Okay. Just relax." Levi closed his eyes and pressed his hands together. After a moment of collecting himself, he ran his fingers down either side of her spine. It didn't take long for him to find the area she'd strained, and then suddenly, the pain seemed to melt away.

"Whoa. That's incredible," Amelia said, testing out a breath and smiling when she felt nothing but relief. "How did you do that?"

"Levi is a very gifted witch," Silas said with an air of reverence.

Amelia rolled over on her back again to find Levi's face tinged pink. She smiled up at the curly-haired teenager with the kind brown eyes and clasped her hand over his. "You really are. Thank you."

"I'm just happy I was able to help. And don't worry about your daughter. She's perfect."

Tears stung Amelia's eyes, and when she pushed herself up into a sitting position without one ounce of pain, she wrapped her arms around him and pulled him in for a hug. "You're a treasure, you know that?"

"Thank you." His voice was muffled in her hair, making her laugh.

When Amelia let him go, she glanced over at Silas. "You got a good one. Make sure you hold on tight."

"I intend to." Silas held his hand out to Levi and pulled him up to sit next to him on the couch. After draping one arm over Levi's shoulders, he whispered in the young man's ear and then kissed him on the cheek.

Amelia pressed her hand to her chest. "Goodness, you two are too sweet for words."

They both chuckled and watched as Grayson helped Amelia to her feet and then pressed a kiss to her temple as he handed her the mug. "I know you feel better, but drink this anyway. If there's any inflammation left over, this will help."

She took a sip and was pleasantly surprised to find the ginger wasn't too overpowering and she actually liked his concoction. "This is pretty good."

When she turned back to the boys on her couch, they were both shifting their gazes from her to Grayson and back.

"What?" she asked.

"Nothing," Silas said, trying to hide a smirk as Levi said, "He's the father of your baby."

Amelia blinked at him, completely taken aback. "How did you know that?"

"She has his energy signature." Levi sat back into the couch and scrunched his face up in embarrassment. "Sorry. That just flew out. I shouldn't have invaded your privacy like that."

"It's all right," Amelia said with a nervous chuckle. "Though I am wondering what else you know about us."

He laughed. "Nothing. It's just because I was so focused on your energy while I worked on your muscle strain. I'm not reading your mind or anything."

"That's too bad," Silas teased as he waved a finger between Grayson and Amelia. "Because there's a story here. I can feel it."

It was Grayson's turn to let out a nervous laugh. "It's not that intriguing. You know, boy meets girl. Boy falls for girl. Boy knocks girl up, leaves town, and then after he tracks her down, he has to convince her to trust him again."

"Oh, that's definitely intriguing," Silas said.

"How so?" Amelia asked, fascinated that he seemed so interested.

"It's what hasn't been said actually." He leaned in, pressing his shoulder into Levi's. "The interesting part is why he left and why she's reluctant to forgive him. If they can work through that, then they'll get their happily ever after." He shrugged. "Or at least that's the way it works in the movies."

Levi let out a soft chuckle. "If only life was always like a movie."

"Hey. It worked for us, didn't it?" Silas insisted.

His boyfriend shrugged one shoulder. "I guess."

Amelia stared at Grayson, knowing that Silas was one hundred percent on the mark. Their story really was in the details and their pasts. The problem was, neither of them had been willing to share their past with each other. They were both flying blind, and it didn't take a genius to realize that without understanding those parts of each other, their relationship was likely to implode before it even began.

CHAPTER 6

By midday, the snow had accumulated another couple of feet, but had finally stopped coming down. Amelia and Silas were in the kitchen making a stew and homemade rolls for dinner, while Cappy, the golden retriever puppy, was curled up in the corner snoozing.

Grayson, itching to do something, recruited Levi to help him shovel the snow from the porch so that they could get to the wood storage and to clear the driveway so Grayson could get out once the snow removal crews arrived to clear the road.

When they were finished, Grayson went inside to grab them both some coffee and returned with Cappy at his heals. The dog ran down the stairs and spun around in the snow, while Grayson sat on the steps with Levi, both of them grateful for the warm drink.

"Thanks for the help," Grayson said.

"No problem. It was good to move a bit. I don't enjoy being cooped up."

"Me neither," Grayson said, suddenly remembering some dark days as a child when he'd been locked up in the house, forbidden to play with the neighborhood children. How many winter days had he sat at the window wishing desperately to be running through the fresh snow or building a snowman with the other kids? But his foster mother hadn't wanted the wet mess that always came with kids running around outside, so instead, she forced them to either sit quietly or do chores to earn television time in the scary basement where her husband ruled the domain.

Grayson could still see the slightly overweight man sitting in the dark with his beer can in one hand and a cigarette in the other as he watched over the kids desperate for their cartoons. He'd never said anything, just watched. But the sinister energy that radiated from him had sent a bolt of fear through Grayson that he'd never forgotten.

Levi shifted beside him and cleared his throat. "Is everything all right?"

Grayson twisted to look at the young man. "Yeah. Of course. Why wouldn't it be?"

"You just..." He shook his head. "Your energy has a signature. Light, kind of inviting. But suddenly it sort of felt heavy, and... I don't know. That usually means someone is upset." Levi grimaced and gave him a pained look. "Never mind. Sorry. It's none of my business. I shouldn't have said anything."

"Don't worry about it," Grayson said automatically as he got to his feet, needing to not feel so exposed. Levi was correct. He was upset. It was rare he let himself think about those days when he lived on Elk Street before Kira had moved in next door and he'd finally had someone who cared about him. "I've got an idea. Why don't we build Amelia a snowman?"

Levi laughed. "Really? Why?"

Grayson shrugged. "It will give us something to do so that we're not sitting around the house. Besides, it's fun, right?"

"If you say so." Levi got to his feet, pulled on his gloves, and the pair of them went to work, gathering snow for their project while Cappy continued to wear himself out by chasing imaginary snowballs. It didn't take long for them to get really into it and start working on making a snow family of two adults and a child between them.

When they were almost done, Levi stood back, inspecting their work. "You know, I never did this as a kid."

There was a sadness in his tone that Grayson related to. "Me neither. Seems crazy since I grew up in Massachusetts."

Levi's eyebrows flew up. "Really? Wow. I grew up here in California, but it didn't snow much in our town. And the few times it did, I wasn't really in a place to do much other than just survive."

Grayson glanced at him. "Sounds rough."

He shrugged. "It was. My dad kicked me out, and the only place I had to go was my uncle's. He wasn't a good man. Life was pretty bad until the universe brought Hope into my life. It's been better since then."

"Sounds familiar," Grayson said, stifling his questions about Levi's life. There were some things that were better left unsaid. He was all too familiar with the pain of reliving past trauma. He'd be damned if he made Levi feel obligated to talk about it.

"Were you homeless, too?" Levi asked, sounding surprised.

"Foster home," he said matter-of-factly. "It was awful… until Kira moved in next door. She made things better."

Levi nodded but didn't say anything. He didn't need to. They understood each other.

"I think they need scarves," Grayson said suddenly. "Give them some color."

"Yeah. Seems like a good idea," Levi said as he secured twigs in place as arms for the snowpeople.

"I have scarves," Amelia said from behind them.

Startled, Grayson turned around, finding her near the porch steps with Cappy already on the porch jumping up on her legs for attention. She reached down and petted the pup, completely unfazed by the wet dog. "Amelia," he said with a nervous laugh. "How long have you been standing there?"

"Not long," she said with a soft smile, making him wonder how much she'd heard of their conversation. "I just wanted to let you guys know the stew is ready." She nodded toward the snow family. "Nice work."

"We're very proud of ourselves," Grayson said, grinning at her.

"Yeah. This might be master-level sculpting," Levi added.

Amelia laughed. "I'd give you the blue ribbon, but you're gonna need those scarves first." She jerked her head toward the front door. "Come in, get something to eat, and then you can dress your snowpeople."

The two men followed Amelia and the dog inside, and after cleaning up, they all sat at her table for dinner. Cappy jumped up on Silas, but when Silas ordered him to sit, his little butt hit the floor obediently. And after Silas gave him a small treat, the puppy flattened out like a ragdoll near his feet.

"Impressive," Amelia said.

He gave a half shrug. "The set I was just on had a trainer. She did most of the work."

"Don't let him fool you, Amelia," Levi said. "He spends more time with Cappy than anyone else. I'm not sure who has who wrapped around their finger… or I guess paw. Because Cappy is spoiled rotten, but also will do anything for him. Me? Forget it." He let out a soft chuckle and shook his head.

"Good thing he's so cute, otherwise we'd have had words by now."

They all laughed and dug into dinner.

"This smells delicious," Grayson said, his stomach grumbling from hunger. "Silas, do you cook much at home?"

The actor shook his head. "There's not a lot of time these days. But I do like the feeling of making something with my own two hands. When I'm on a job, it's mostly takeout. It's only when I'm here with Levi that I seem to have time for homecooked meals." He reached over and squeezed his boyfriend's hand before adding, "Unfortunately, that doesn't happen as often as I'd like."

"He's only been home for a few days," Levi said, his eyes firmly on his stew. "Soon he has to go back to Canada to finish a film."

"I'll be back in March," Silas said, his voice full of forced cheer.

"March thirtieth," Levi said. "Six weeks this time." There was no mistaking the bitterness in his voice.

Silas sighed. "I know. It's too long, but I don't really have a choice. You could come visit me."

Levi nodded and pushed the stew around in his bowl.

Grayson, having been in Levi's shoes more than once, gave the kid a sympathetic smile. "At least you won't have to deal with invasive paparazzi, uncomfortable beds, and bland food from craft service."

Silas eyed him. "You sound like you've acted before."

"Me?" Grayson asked, surprised. "Oh no. I... uh, I dated someone in the business for a while. There was a lot to dislike about celebrity, but the worst was the lack of privacy. Nobody should be subjected to that level of scrutiny."

"Amen to that," Silas said, raising his root beer glass.

"You did?" Amelia asked, her eyes wide. "Who?"

Shit. What had he been thinking? This was why he never talked about Kira. It was too easy to slip up. What was he supposed to say? That he had an NDA with the one person who'd ever cared about him? It was the truth, but saying it made him feel like he needed to vomit. He grimaced and went with the practiced lie he'd told over the years when he found himself in this exact position. "It was someone in Katy Carmichael's circle. Her name was Kira." It was almost the truth. Sort of.

Silas frowned. "What roles has she played?"

"She did some uncredited work," he lied. "Modeling was her main gig. Mostly runway and catalog stuff. But because she was part of Katy's group, I got a front row view of the celebrity life. It wasn't pretty." In fact, as soon as Katy's star began to rise, that was the beginning of the end for them. It wasn't a life Grayson was suited for.

"It can be pretty brutal," Silas said.

"For the ones left behind," Levi said bitterly and got to his feet. He placed his cloth napkin on the table, muttered his thanks, and took off for the back door.

"Levi!" Silas called. "Where are you going?"

"Out. I just need a minute." Silas started to go after him, but Levi shook his head and said, "Don't. Not now."

Silas sat back down and slumped in his chair. He squeezed his eyes shut and muttered, "Dammit."

"He'll come around," Grayson said softly. "I don't know him well, but after spending the afternoon with him, it's pretty clear he really cares about you."

"I know he does, but we have so little time together right now, and I just don't know if he's going to find a way to be okay with it," Silas said with a sigh. He stared at the back door where Levi had disappeared, the desire to go after him clear in his expression. "I was supposed to be here for six weeks and then take off to do another movie, but the job got moved up, and now I'm supposed to leave tomorrow. I asked him to come visit me, but he has his own thing here with healer Snow. Plus, money is an issue. He doesn't like it when I pay for everything."

"That's understandable," Grayson said softly. "It's hard being away from the one you love. It's even harder feeling like you have nothing to contribute." Grayson identified with Levi more than he could admit.

"I know. I just don't know what to do about it." Silas met Amelia's gaze. "Will you go after him? Make sure he's okay?"

"Of course." She squeezed Silas's hand, bundled herself into a jacket, and slipped outside.

"Can I give you some advice from someone who has been in Levi's shoes?" Grayson asked.

"I'm all ears, man," Silas said, looking pained. "Levi is the most important person in my life."

Grayson nodded. "I can see that you really care about him. Here's the thing… You're young, so I'm sure that everyone around you is telling you that you have to make decisions for what is best for you personally, not your relationship."

"Yeah. No one expects us to last. Even my sister, Shannon, who is great and loves Levi, is always telling me that he can't factor into my career decisions."

"And she's right. Mostly. But I'm guessing that when she says that she's probably not factoring in your needs *outside* of your career," Grayson said.

Silas frowned. "I don't think that's true. Shannon loves me and is always careful to support my decisions. If I don't want to do a project, she always backs me up even if everyone else thinks it's the right career move."

"That's good. You're lucky to have her. Not all young stars have someone like that in their corner. But that's different than really knowing what you need in here." Grayson tapped his chest. "I'm not saying you should prioritize your relationship with Levi over your career, especially if he's not supportive—"

"Levi's supportive of me. That's not the issue," Silas insisted.

"Great. Glad to hear it. I'm just saying that you need to take care of you, too. If spending time with him is important to you, then make that a priority, because nothing is more important than the people you care about. All the fame and money in the world can't replace that connection you have with the person you love. And worse, if you let it, fame and celebrity can destroy the bond you share. Just don't get too swept up in it all or you could find you have everything in the world except the one person you love most."

Silas stared at him for a long moment. "You sound like a man who speaks from experience."

"You could say that."

"There's more to your story with, what's her name… Kira?" he asked.

"Yes. But that's a tale for another day. Just remember what I said. Levi deserves more than being left behind in a hotel room while you spend eighteen hours a day working on a film."

CHAPTER 7

"Hey there," Amelia said, finding Levi leaning against the railing of her back porch.

"Hi." He grimaced. "Sorry I made a scene back there."

"You didn't make a scene. You're just upset." She took up residence against the railing next to him. "Do you want to talk about it?"

"What's there to say?" He stared out at the snow blanketing her property. "Silas's career is taking off in a major way. I can't compete with that."

"Here's the good news," she said, giving him a soft smile. "You don't need to compete. That's not what relationships are about."

"*Some* relationships. He's never here. Not anymore. Four days. That's all I get, and then he's gone again, doing I don't even know what."

Amelia frowned. "Are you afraid he's with someone else when he's away?"

Levi's eyes widened. "No. Not at all. He's just... always busy with no time to even video chat. It's really hard."

Amelia reached out and squeezed his hand. "That does sound challenging. I guess what you have to ask yourself is if he's worth waiting for."

"Of course he is." He pulled his hand from hers and ran it through his hair in frustration. "I just don't know how much longer he's going to think that *I'm* worth it."

"Oh, Levi," Amelia said gently. "I don't think he's suddenly going to stop caring about you. But your fears are valid, and that's something you two should probably sit down and talk about. Tell him how you're feeling so you can deal with it together."

"I can't do that," he said, his eyes wide as he glanced around as if Silas was going to appear right in front of him. "He doesn't need that kind of pressure. Besides, what if he tells me he thinks this is too hard and ends it? I'm…" He shook his head. "I'm not ready for that."

She chuckled softly.

His head jerked up and he narrowed his eyes at her. "Why are you laughing?"

"Honey, if I had to guess, I'd say you're the one person Silas never wants to cut loose. I've listened to him talk about Hollywood all day. And from the sounds of it, he's not really into any of it except for the actual art of acting. Looks to me like you're his sanctuary away from all the drama. I know you're worried about the future and the time you get together, but just talk to him, okay?"

Levi didn't exactly look convinced, but he nodded. And a moment later, he followed her back into the house.

Silas jumped up from the table with Cappy scrambling after him. "Levi, I—I'm sorry." He wrapped his arms around the other young man and whispered something in his ear.

"Come on," Amelia said, taking Grayson's hand and tugging him toward the living room. "Let's give them a minute."

"Is Levi okay?" Grayson asked, his tone more concerned than curious as he lowered himself onto the couch.

"I think he will be if they can find a way to discuss their fears," Amelia said as she sat in her oversized chair.

"I see." Grayson frowned, and a small crease formed between his eyes. "That could be harder than you might think."

Amelia raised her eyebrows in surprise. "Why? They both seem like honest kids."

"Honesty isn't the problem." Grayson strummed his fingers on his knee. "It's courage. Levi has pretty classic abandonment issues. With Silas gone a lot, it's going to be a recurring problem."

"What makes you think that?" she asked curiously.

"Just a conversation we had today. Levi and I have a lot in common."

"You both have abandonment issues?" she asked, shocked. It was the first time Grayson had even come close to alluding to anything personal in his life.

"Um, this was supposed to be about Levi," he said quietly.

Her frustration welled up in her chest, making it difficult to breathe. How was she supposed to have any sort of relationship with him if he never opened up about anything? "Sounds like Levi isn't the one with a courage problem. How am I supposed to trust you if you never tell me anything?"

His dark eyes narrowed, and his shoulders tensed. He looked as if he was ready to flee, only there was nowhere for him to go. "Is this really how you want to do this, Amelia?"

"No. Not at all." She stood, guilt eating away at her gut. Had she really sat there and tried to push him into talking about something he clearly didn't want to discuss? "I'm sorry. I shouldn't have said that." She covered her face with her hands and let out a small groan. "It's just that I don't know anything about your past at all. It makes me feel like I don't know the father of my child. And I'm not saying this to manipulate you into telling me things you don't want to talk about. I'm just explaining myself. You said you want me to trust you, but you clearly don't trust me." She shook her head and added, "It's been a long day. I'm going to go lie down. Tell Levi and Silas they are welcome to stay the night if they want."

Grayson didn't say anything as she walked down the hall to her bedroom. Once safely inside, she leaned against the door and muttered a curse. She hadn't wanted to fight with Grayson. And she definitely didn't want to push him into confiding in her. He'd implied abandonment. Likely some kind of trauma. That wasn't something a person just blurted out.

What was wrong with her?

She already knew the answer to that question. Amelia was still hurt that he'd abandoned her. She'd given him her heart, and he'd left her with nothing but a surprise pregnancy. It was enough to make any girl go slightly insane.

"Get it together, Amelia," she scolded herself. "You can't keep punishing him for something he had every right to do." He'd never promised her anything. They'd both said the relationship was casual. She'd been the one to break the rules by falling for him. And now she was continuing to punish him for not feeling the same way. It wasn't right, and she needed to let it go once and for all.

Disappointed in herself, she changed into a set of satin pajamas and crawled into bed. She laid there for a while, staring up at the ceiling until the gray evening light turned to darkness. Eventually she fell into a fitful sleep and was transported back eighteen years, to a drizzly day at a mountain lake.

THE DREAM STARTED *the way it always did. Victoria was sitting on the dock, her feet dangling over the edge, holding an unlit cigarette.*

"You're not going to smoke that, are you?" Amelia asked, crinkling her nose at the offending object.

"Of course I am. Why else would I snitch it from Madison's purse?" She flicked the striker of the lighter a few times, watching it spark but not catch.

Madison was her father's third wife and was only six years older than the two friends. At twenty-one, Victoria's newest stepmother was twenty-three years younger than her husband. "She's going to tell your dad," Amelia said.

"He won't care," she said with a roll of her eyes. This time the flame flickered to life, and she placed the cigarette between her lips as she sucked in air and expertly lit the stolen Marlboro Red. After expelling the smoke from her lungs, she added, "As long as I don't bother them when they disappear into his bedroom to fuck, he doesn't give a shit what I do."

The vitriol in her voice made Amelia recoil. She hadn't ever heard her friend talk like that before. It wasn't the foul language that shocked her, it was the pure disgust aimed at her father. Victoria's mother died when she was a baby, leaving her dad to be her sole parent. The two had been inseparable, and Victoria idolized him. Nothing had changed between them when he'd married Carol three years earlier, and Amelia thought Victoria had gotten the family she'd always wanted.

Then the shit had hit the fan.

Carol had caught her dad cheating with Madison just over a year ago, and their lives blew up. Victoria was devastated when Carol left and downright defiant when Madison moved in. But now? She sounded bitter and angry and not at all like the happy, carefree girl Amelia had been best friends with since the first grade.

"Do you want to stay over at our place tonight? I'm with my mom this week," Amelia offered. "It's pancake night."

Victoria shook her head. "No. I have plans with Craig Baxton. He's taking me to the hill."

"What?" Amelia leaned in, scenting the foul stench of the cigarette and coughing before whispering, "Does your dad know?"

"Of course not." Victoria looked at her like she'd lost her mind. "Why would I tell him? He'd just tell me Craig is too old for me. Like he has any room to talk about age. Twenty-three years is a hell of a lot more offensive than four."

Amelia had to admit that her friend had a point. Except nineteen seemed so much older than their fifteen years. Craig had already graduated and was in college, while Amelia and Victoria were freshmen in high school. "I heard he took Candy to the hill last week."

Victoria's eyes flashed with irritation. "Why would you tell me that?"

"Because I thought you should know. That's why," Amelia shot back. "You know he only wants to take you there for one thing. How are you going to feel when he's there with someone else next week?"

"Did you ever stop and think that maybe I know what I'm doing?" Victoria asked.

"Um, no," Amelia answered honestly. She was far too worried about her friend to hold back. "Because if you did, you'd know he's just going to sleep with you and then never talk to you again. Honestly, Vic, what else would he be taking a freshman out for? Why wouldn't he be dating college girls? Don't you think it's strange that he's interested in you when there's a giant campus full of girls his own age?"

"You want to know something?" Victoria said, her voice dead calm as she got to her feet.

"What?" Amelia stood to face her friend, and nerves took over, making her stomach ache. She knew whatever Victoria was going to say would be something she didn't want to hear.

"I came on to Craig. I asked him to take me to the hill. I want him to fuck me." Her bottom lip trembled, and tears filled her eyes as she added, "Then maybe I'll understand."

Amelia sucked in a sharp breath. "Victoria," she said softly. "No. You don't want to do this." She reached out to pull her friend into a hug, but Victoria shook her head and jerked back suddenly.

Victoria's foot slipped on the edge of the dock, and just like that, she went over the side, but not before there was a loud crack as her head hit the piling.

"Victoria!" Amelia screamed as she watched her friend's body disappear under the murky water. Fear gripped her, and she froze, unable to move as pure horror rooted her to the dock. But then her eyes focused on the water where Victoria had disappeared, and Amelia sucked in a sharp breath. Something about the cool air hitting her lungs snapped her out of her shock, and without any other thought, she dove into the chilly lake, frantically searching for her friend.

Amelia dove down into the water, searching for Victoria. The water was too murky to see anything, so she dove and blindly searched over and over again, even as her entire body went numb from the cold and her teeth chattered. She didn't know how long she was in the water, but she kept screaming her friend's name every time she surfaced, panic-stricken and nearly out of her mind as tears streamed down her face. Eventually, Victoria's father appeared and dragged Amelia out of the water and handed her off to a white-faced Madison while he jumped in the lake himself to search fruitlessly for the daughter he'd already lost.

Amelia broke down and sobbed, lost in her own personal hell, unable to block out the vision of her friend's last moment when she slipped from the dock.

"AMELIA, WAKE UP," a familiar voice whispered in her ear. "It's okay, baby. You're safe." Strong arms wrapped around her, warming her chilled limbs.

"Victoria," Amelia muttered, tasting salty tears on her own lips. "She's gone."

"Shh, it's okay now. You're safe. I promise."

Amelia's eyes flew open, and she stared at the darkened window. Soft light flooded her familiar room, while strong, comforting arms held her from behind.

Grayson. He was in her bed, holding her with one hand resting on her stomach and the other gently combing through her hair. She knew she should pull away from him, but she couldn't. She was still too shaken by the dream. The one she hadn't had in over ten years.

"Oh, gods," she breathed. "Are Levi and Silas still here?" She was going to die if they'd heard her screaming in her sleep.

"Yes. I gave them the guest room and moved to the nursery. It's snowing again and the roads still haven't been plowed."

She groaned. "How loud was I?"

"Loud enough," he whispered. "But don't worry about it. Everyone has nightmares sometimes." He pressed a light kiss to her temple.

"Not like that," she said, closing her eyes, just taking a moment to be comforted by being in his arms again. She knew she shouldn't, considering their relationship was in limbo, but she was too shaken up to care at the moment.

"Do you want to talk about it?" There wasn't any

expectation in his tone, and she got the distinct impression that if she said no, he'd leave it alone. Something she hadn't been able to do earlier. *Dammit.*

"Yeah," she said, surprised by her answer. She rarely talked about Victoria anymore. The trauma just never went away. A therapist had helped her find ways to cope, but thinking about her beautiful friend and remembering that last day was always rough. But now that she was having the dream again, she knew talking was the only way to settle her mind. If she didn't talk about it, she would likely have the same dream until she found the courage to face it again.

"Okay. I'm here," he said, tucking a strand of her hair behind her ear as he ran his knuckles gently over her cheek.

He was being too tender. Too caring. It was enough to break her heart all over again. She rolled over to face him, wanting to see his face as she talked. He placed one hand on her hip, keeping the connection between them, and he gave her a reassuring smile.

"When I was fifteen, I was there when my best friend slipped off the end of a dock, hit her head on a piling, and disappeared into the lake. Three days passed before they found her body."

He sucked in a sharp breath. "That's really awful, Amelia. I'm so sorry. Nobody should have to live through something like that, especially at the age of fifteen."

"You're right," she said. "It was the single worst day of my life."

CHAPTER 8

Grayson wanted to gather Amelia in his arms and somehow absorb all of the trauma she'd suffered that fateful day when she'd lost her friend. He was no stranger to that sort of pain, and if it were possible, he'd gladly shoulder the burden of hers.

"I don't really remember jumping into the lake," Amelia said. "I know it happened, because I dream about it, but as far as recalling it from my personal memory... That just isn't here."

"It was a traumatic event," Grayson said, his heart breaking for her younger self. He'd witnessed plenty of awful events during his formative years and understood better than most what she'd gone through. "It makes sense that your subconscious has hidden it from you."

"I don't really remember anything other than I couldn't stop looking for her." Amelia's voice was barely a whisper. "I was in the water for two hours. Two hours, Grayson. And I don't think I would have stopped searching for her if Victoria's father hadn't hauled me out of the lake." There were unshed tears in her eyes. Her voice broke as she added, "I couldn't give up on her."

A single tear fell down her cheek, and Grayson reached out to stop it with his thumb.

She closed her eyes and sucked in a shaky breath. "It's been a long time since I had that dream. I just don't know why it's back now."

Grayson let his instincts take over and gathered her in his arms. He pulled her close as he lay on his back, positioning her so that her head lay on his chest. He idly ran his fingers up and down the tender skin of her neck, hoping that his touch soothed her.

"She was the best friend I ever had… and then she was gone. How does anyone get over that?"

"I doubt you do," he said. "You just need to find ways to cope."

She sighed. "I guess."

Silence fell between them, but it was that quiet space between two people who didn't need words.

Grayson wished again with everything he had that he could take the pain away for her. He'd gladly hold on to it and stash it away with his own past trauma if it meant she didn't have to suffer again. But he knew that there was no easing someone else's pain.

"I'm sorry," she said.

"There's nothing to be sorry for, Amelia," he said, kissing the top of her head and tightening his hold on her.

"Yes, there is." Her voice was stronger now as she tilted her head up to look him in the eye. "We had an agreement, and I broke it."

He frowned. "What are you talking about?"

"That weekend we spent in Cape Cod. The night I told you

I love you. That was a mistake. I shouldn't have done that."

A sharp pain shot through his chest at the idea that she thought it was a mistake to love him. He grimaced. Of course she did. Look at how he'd behaved. He needed to say something. To make this right between them. "It's never a mistake to tell someone how you feel."

She nodded, her silky hair tickling his neck. "I agree. After I lost Victoria, I made a promise to myself that I wouldn't hold back. That I'd tell the people I cared about how I felt, because life is just too short. You never know what will happen. So I'm not sorry for that." Amelia pushed herself up and stared down at him in the darkness. "I'm sorry for getting upset when my declaration wasn't returned. I knew that you weren't looking for anything serious or permanent. I had no right to expect you to reciprocate my feelings."

Oh hell, Grayson thought. The words he'd desperately wanted to say then were still clogged in his throat. Only this time, it wasn't just fear that had him swallowing his emotions. If he managed to get those words out now, it would feel wrong. Like he'd only said them because she was vulnerable, or because she was pregnant and he felt he had to say it in order to be part of their lives. Neither of those things were true of course, but the timing was all wrong. They needed time to get to a place where they were both ready for those words.

Instead, he tugged her back down and gave her a part of himself he'd never given anyone else. Not even Kira. "When I was a kid, my parents used to take me to Sugarloaf every Christmas. They had me later in life, and both sets of my grandparents had already passed, so it was just the three of us."

"You only have your parents?" she asked, sounding astonished that he was talking about his past at all. She likely had no idea just how hard this was for him. "No siblings? I thought you had a brother in Pennsylvania or something."

"Foster brother," he corrected, his voice cracking with the admission. "And no, no other siblings."

She stared up at him, her eyes full of understanding. Grayson expected her to ask more questions or say something awkward the way people always seemed to when they realized he was an orphan. But she didn't. She just waited patiently, appearing to understand that he'd get everything out in his own time.

"They rented a condo near the slopes, and we skied straight through Christmas. I learned to ski not long after I could walk, and up until I was ten years old, that was our little family tradition instead of having a big family gathering for the holidays."

"That sounds wonderful," Amelia said, squeezing his hand.

"Memories of those trips are the only thing that got me through the next eight years of my life." His throat got tight, and he had to pause to let the painful emotions pass. "The Christmas that I turned ten, we had a great holiday on the mountain, but we ended up needing to leave a day early because Dad got called into work. It had snowed that day, and I remember Mom being nervous about the road conditions. But Dad's boss was clear; he needed to be there, or they'd hand off his biggest account to someone else. So we piled in the car to head home."

Was that a hitch in his voice? He wasn't sure because there was a ringing in his ears. He ignored the noise and forced himself to continue. "There was a lot of traffic and a few accidents that kept us on the road longer than usual. And when night fell, ice formed on the highway. We were just a few miles from home when Dad hit a patch of ice, and we hit another car head-on."

Amelia let out a gasp, clutching him tighter. "You were in that car," she whispered.

"In the backseat. They used the Jaws of Life to get me out. I had a compound fracture in my leg, a broken wrist, and some internal injuries. Both of my parents died on impact."

Tears streamed down Amelia's face, and Grayson had to look away as his eyes stung with his own tears.

"After I got out of the hospital, I was sent to a foster home." He forced himself to look at her and to wipe her tears away, even as his own fell unchecked down his cheeks. "I just wanted you to know that I understand your grief. You're not alone in this pain, and if there is anything I can do to help ease yours, I will."

"Grayson," she breathed and pressed her entire body against his. "I'm so sorry."

"I know." He ran his hand over her hair. "So am I."

She entwined her fingers with his and asked, "Am I allowed to ask what happened after you were placed in the foster home?"

He stiffened. "I don't—"

"You don't have to talk about it," she said quickly. "I'm sure there are reasons why you've never said anything about it before."

"There are," he said, briefly considering leaving the conversation there, but for some strange reason, he wanted to tell her the rest. Or at least the condensed version of it.

"I understand," she said.

He gave her a gentle smile, thankful that she wasn't pushing. It somehow made it easier to share. "I was in that foster home until I turned eighteen. It wasn't a good place. So bad in fact, that the day I turned eighteen, I left and never looked back."

"How?"

"My parents had a college fund for me. It wasn't a lot, but it was enough to pay for two years. I worked and took out loans for the rest." He'd left a lot out of his explanation, but everything he'd said was true.

"I can't imagine what that must have been like for you," she said, reaching up to cup his cheek. "I wish I could've been there for you then."

He took her palm and kissed it. "Thank you. Everything that I just told you is why I will never abandon you and our child. My family was taken away from me. I won't walk away from this one."

Fresh tears filled her eyes, spilling silently down her cheeks. She opened her mouth to say something but then shut it again and just hugged him tight.

Before long, they fell asleep like that, with Amelia in his arms. And for the first time in his life since that disastrous day when he'd lost his parents, he felt like he'd come home.

CHAPTER 9

Amelia woke early, the weak February sun spilling in her window. Grayson lay beside her, his arm wrapped around her middle, holding her close. They were both still fully clothed and, as near as she could tell, once she'd finally fallen back to sleep the night before, neither of them had moved once.

She carefully slipped from his hold and disappeared into her bathroom. Ten minutes later, she left him sleeping and padded to the kitchen to find her houseguests with their arms around each other as they laughed at something. Cappy, the golden puppy, sat at their feet, staring adoringly up at them. She grinned at them. "Well, hello."

"Good morning," Silas said, letting go of Levi as his eyes twinkled and a huge smile broke out on his face.

"Morning." Levi flushed pink and gave her a smile of his own. It was clear the pair had worked out their differences for the moment at least.

Amelia glanced around at the breakfast they'd made. "What's all this?"

"A thank you for… everything," Silas said. "We weren't sure what you and Grayson liked, so we made a little bit of everything." He gestured to the eggs, bacon, pancakes, and toast.

"Wow. You didn't have to do all of that. But it looks wonderful. Thank you." She reached for her coffee pot, but Levi beat her to it.

"I've got this. Take a seat. I'll bring it to you." He went to work, making a fresh pot while Silas held out a chair for her to sit.

"Decaf please. You guys are really going all out. Really, you didn't need to do this," she said. "You two are welcome here anytime."

Silas and Levi glanced at each other, a silent communication passing between them before Silas sat beside her and said, "It's not just the hospitality. The advice you and Grayson gave us… Well, let's just say we worked some things out."

Amelia watched as they smiled almost shyly at each other. It had been an emotional night for her and Grayson, but the two young men in her kitchen filled her heart with joy. The love between them was undeniable. They really were young, but she truly hoped that they managed to make what they had last. "I'm really happy to hear that."

"So am I," Grayson said, appearing in the doorway wearing his wool pants and a white T-shirt. He looked gorgeous with his hair slightly mussed and a two-day beard. His gaze landed on Amelia, and the tender look on his face made her insides melt.

"Morning," they all said in unison.

He chuckled. "Morning. What's going on in here?"

"Breakfast," Silas said, handing him a mug of coffee.

"Thanks, man."

After Levi passed Amelia her coffee, the two young men stepped back, and Levi said, "We're going to head out."

"Is the power back on?" Amelia asked.

Silas shrugged. "I'm not sure. But they cleared the road, so if it's not, I'll get packed and then we'll head to Levi's place."

Amelia got up and hugged Levi first. And then when she hugged Silas, she said, "I'm glad we got a chance to get to know you. I'm sorry you're leaving so soon. If you want me to keep an eye on your place, just say the word."

"Levi will be there part of the time, but yes. I'd love it if you'd keep an eye on things, especially if there's a storm."

"I'm happy to do it."

Grayson rose and shook both of their hands. "Do good work," he told Silas. "And when you're done, remember what's most important."

He nodded solemnly, and then the two took off with Cappy at their heels.

"I really like them," Amelia said, nibbling on a piece of toast.

"They're good kids," Grayson agreed.

"Kids." Amelia chuckled. "I know they are still teenagers, but they are the most mature teenagers I've ever met."

"That happens when one lives an entire lifetime before they're even a legal adult." He took a sip of his coffee. "Levi was on his own for a while, and Silas… Didn't he basically divorce his parents because they were controlling every aspect of his career?"

"Yes, I think so. It's why he lives in Keating Hollow and Shannon is his manager now," Amelia said.

"That's a lot of crap to deal with when you're still just a kid. It makes sense they'd want stability."

"It does," she agreed, and somehow, she inherently knew

that he wasn't just talking about Levi and Silas now. He was reiterating what he'd told her the night before. They might have started their relationship strictly casual, with no strings attached, but that was a thing of the past. Grayson had moved beyond his fear of commitment and was all in. However, as much as she'd wanted to hear those words, things were moving too fast for her to process. "Grayson, we need to talk."

He put his fork down and sat back in his chair, giving her a concerned look. "Is something wrong?"

She shook her head. "No. It's just that I feel like we went from zero to two hundred in five seconds flat. Two days ago, you didn't even know about the baby, and we weren't anything to each other. Now you're talking about being all in this with me." She waved a hand between them. "Whatever *this* is."

He frowned. "I thought that's what you wanted."

"It was. I mean, I do," she stammered. "I just don't know what we are to each other except for the fact that we share this baby." She pressed a hand to her abdomen protectively. "I get that you want to be here for your child. And while last night was… kind of intense for both of us, I don't know where we stand."

"What exactly are you saying, Amelia? Are you asking if we're in a relationship? Because if so, then my answer is yes. I have zero intention of dating anyone else. You're… well, you're *you* and the mother of my child. I'm *in* this with you."

She let out a chuckle and gave him a small smile. "I know. But I think we might be going too fast for me. Can we take a step back maybe? Use the next few months to get to know each other. Go out on some dates. And then if we're both still on the same page, we can define whatever this is going to be?"

Grayson let out a sigh of relief and gave her a chuckle of his own. "Yes. I'd love to date you. How about tonight? After I go home, shower and shave, find some clean clothes, I could take you to Woodlines or the Cozy Cave. Or even the brewery if you prefer."

The tension she'd woken up with in her shoulders immediately eased, and she nodded enthusiastically. "Woodlines. It's my favorite. But don't shave. I really love that beard growth."

His lips twitched into a half-smile, and he winked. "Got it. Sexy two-day beard it is."

∼

AMELIA MEANDERED AROUND HER HOUSE, changing the sheets in the guest room, straightening the living room, and finally ending up in the kitchen making a banana bread with the brown bananas in her counter basket. She'd needed to keep busy, because after Grayson left, for the first time ever, Amelia's sanctuary on the hill felt empty. She'd always enjoyed her solitude after growing up with a large extended family. But now? She missed the easy company of Silas, Levi, and Grayson.

Grayson, she thought with a sigh.

The dynamic between them had changed the night before. They'd been vulnerable with each other, and now she felt an emotional connection to him that had been missing. She now knew why he was so hesitant to get close to anyone, and she could understand why he'd run when they'd gotten too close. All she could do was hope that he meant it when he'd said he wasn't going anywhere and that he wanted this family. She wasn't expecting a marriage proposal, but she did hope they could start over and build some sort of stable life for their daughter.

"Hello?" Holly called, startling Amelia out of her thoughts.

"In here," Amelia called from the kitchen. She rinsed her hands under the tap and wiped them with a towel as Rex and Holly strode in wearing wide smiles, their faces flushed from the cold.

"Hey, Sis," Rex said, kissing her cheek. "You doing okay after being holed up here for a few days?"

"Of course," she said, waving her hand dismissively. "Why wouldn't I be?"

He glanced around and shrugged one shoulder. "No reason. I know you're more than capable of taking care of yourself, but that doesn't mean I won't worry when I know you're snowed in with no way off the mountain if things go south."

Amelia rolled her eyes, choosing to let his comment go. She was a full-grown adult who'd lived through her fair share of snowstorms. "How was your weekend at the inn?"

Holly flushed bright red as she leaned into Rex, hugging him from the side. Then she turned shyly to Amelia. "It was a wonderful Valentine's Day getaway."

"That's good," Amelia said softly, pleased for them both. Her brother had spent far too many years alone after his previous fiancée had screwed him over in the worst way possible. Rex deserved to be happy with someone like Holly. Someone who loved him deeply and didn't have a cruel or ugly bone in her body.

"I just wish you and I could've had more time together," Holly said, moving toward Amelia with her arms outstretched for a hug. "I was really looking forward to spending some time with you and doing a lot more baby shopping to fill that nursery. Unfortunately, Rex needs to get me home so I can go into work tomorrow."

Amelia hugged the other woman fiercely. "I was looking

forward to that, too. But we still have time. Let's set a date to get together again soon."

"Definitely." Holly kissed Amelia's cheek and then disappeared from the kitchen, leaving Amelia and Rex alone.

Rex stared at his sister, his blue eyes troubled.

"Just ask me whatever it is you need to ask me," Amelia said with a sigh.

"I'm just worried about you." He took her hand and led her to the table where they sat down.

"Why? I'm fine. I do know how to handle a snowstorm, you know." She couldn't stop the irritation from coming through in her voice. But when she saw the hurt look on his face, she softened her tone. "I'm not fifteen anymore, Rex."

"Of course you aren't. But you're my baby sister, and I can't help worrying. What happened with Grayson?"

She knew he'd ask. He was, after all, the person she'd run to after Grayson had left her in December. "We talked. He wants to be a part of our lives, so tonight we're going out to dinner to try to start over."

"Start over? You mean you're dating again? Just like that?"

"You don't have to sound so judgmental," she said, rolling her eyes.

"I'm not being judgmental. Dammit, Amelia, I just don't want to see you get hurt again."

She reached over and squeezed his hand lightly. "I know you don't. I don't want that either, but it's a risk I'm willing to take. Because the truth is, he's my baby's father, I still love him, and he wants to be a part of our lives. So what choice do I have other than to give this a try?"

Rex let out an impatient grunt. "You trust too easily."

"And you don't trust enough," she said, not unkindly. "But I think Holly might be helping with that."

He glanced past her toward the hallway where Holly had disappeared a few moments earlier. "She's one of a kind."

"She loves you."

He smiled and his expression went soft in a way that Amelia had never really seen on her brother before. He was with his ex for years, but he'd never been as happy with her as he was with Holly. "I just got lucky and found my one." His smile vanished as he stared at his sister. "I'm worried that you're attaching yourself to someone who doesn't deserve you."

Anger rose up from the pit of her stomach and she stood, suddenly feeling both insulted that her brother didn't trust her and offended for Grayson. "You don't know him, Rex. I do. Maybe you could trust me and stop acting like no one deserves a second chance. Didn't you leave Holly before coming back and begging her for forgiveness?"

"That's not fair," he said, standing to stare down at her. "I came here to figure stuff out and then went right back. I didn't leave her for months while she was pregnant!"

Amelia glared at her brother and then without another word, she turned on her heel and left the kitchen. When she was halfway down the hallway, Holly stepped out of the small laundry room with a pair of gray sweats and a sweatshirt.

"Amelia?" she asked with a teasing tone in her voice. "Just who exactly do these belong to?"

"Oh. Grayson of course. He must've forgotten to collect them before he left." After his day in the snow with Levi, he'd dumped them in her washer.

"Grayson was *here*?" Rex said from behind her.

"Yes," she said impatiently. "He brought me home and we ended up snowed in together. I told you that."

"No you didn't," they said in unison. Holly's tone was full of interest, while Rex's was just irritated.

"I didn't?" Amelia frowned. "I could've sworn that when I texted, I told you we were snowed in together." She waved a dismissive hand. "It doesn't matter. We used the time to work through some things."

"I bet." Holly's eyes sparkled as she grinned.

"Stop," Amelia said, laughing, pleased at least one of them wasn't being an overbearing jackass. "Levi and Silas were here most of the time, too. Nothing happened."

"If you say so," Holly said, eyeing Amelia's abdomen with a smirk.

"Well, not this weekend anyway." Amelia chuckled, enjoying having someone on her side. "Tell my brother to chill out, will you?" she added. "I think he's getting ready to have an aneurysm."

Holly laughed, handed Amelia the clothes, and then took her man by the arm. "Come on. Give your sister a break and help me pack."

"I'm not going to have an aneurysm," he grumbled, but he let Holly guide him away.

Amelia sent her friend a silent thank you. She knew her brother was just protective, but that didn't mean she was going to let him walk all over her. Her mind was made up. Grayson deserved another chance and that was exactly what he was going to get.

Hours later, Rex and Holly still hadn't left Amelia's house on the hill. Rex had one excuse after another, starting with shoveling the snow off the roof and ending with checking her generator just in case there was another storm.

"You do realize the snow wasn't so thick you needed to

shovel it. And if I have a problem with the generator, I can call someone, right?"

"I just want to make sure my sister is safe. I don't want you to worry about anything other than that baby you're carrying," he said.

Holly snorted. "Don't buy any of that, Amelia. He's just waiting around to talk to Grayson when he comes to pick you up."

Amelia had guessed that was why Rex had become so helpful, but she'd been hoping that if she ignored him, he'd give up and go home. "Rex, Holly has to work tomorrow. Take her home, please."

"I just want to have a word with him," Rex said mildly as he filled a glass of water from the pitcher on her counter.

"Why?" Amelia asked, getting frustrated. "There's nothing to say."

Holly sighed. "I had a vision and made the mistake of sharing it with Mr. Buttinski."

"What vision?" Amelia focused on her.

Holly closed her eyes and shook her head as if she didn't want to get into it. But when the silence became too heavy in the room, she let out a curse and said, "I saw him leaving this house with a suitcase. He had a plane ticket to New York City in his hand. You were... not happy."

Amelia let Holly's words sink in. There was no doubt that it worried her. Holly's visions were solid. Much more reliable than the ones Amelia had been having since she became pregnant. But it wasn't as if Grayson would never travel again. Who was to say that his trip had anything to do with leaving Amelia? If she was going to try to trust him, she needed to give him a chance and not write him off because of visions with no context. She turned to her brother. "Didn't Holly have a vision of you here in Keating Hollow in my nursery that made her believe that you weren't going to stay in Christmas Grove?"

"Yes, but—" he started.

"That's all I needed to hear. This conversation is done, and you two need to get on the road. I won't hear another word about it," Amelia said with her hands on her hips.

Holly nodded, stood, and grabbed Rex by the hand. "I think she won that round." Smiling at him, she added, "Let's go home. I'm ready to try that thing again. You know... the one we tried after the wedding?"

"La, la, la, la!" Amelia said, covering her ears with her hands. "There are some things a sister should never hear."

They were both chuckling as they hugged her goodbye and promised they'd be back soon.

Amelia let out a slow breath, still unsettled by Holly's vision, and then tried her damnedest to put it out of her mind.

CHAPTER 10

Grayson could hardly wait to get back to Amelia. He spent the day trying to go over some spreadsheets of his sales accounts, but the work had been fruitless. He hadn't been able to concentrate. Instead, he'd daydreamed about what it might be like to live with Amelia and the baby in the house with the gorgeous view of the valley. It amazed him how his outlook on life had changed in just a few days. But here he was, headed back up the hill with flowers on the passenger seat and his heart on his sleeve.

He wanted Amelia. There was no doubt about that. He'd always wanted her. He just hadn't felt free enough to give all of himself. He was past that now, and more than that, he wanted the life she promised. The one that had been so cruelly taken from him when he was just a young man.

Light flooded from the front porch and the wide picture window of her home. He smiled to himself as he put the Toyota in park, grabbed the bouquet of white daisies, and jumped out of his SUV.

Before he could even stride up the steps, the door opened

and Amelia stood in the doorway, her natural brown curls framing her face as she smiled at him. She was wearing jeans and a blouse that hugged her breasts, showing off her enticing cleavage. "You look gorgeous," he said, handing her the bouquet.

"Gorgeous is a little over the top, but I'll take it." She turned and glided back into the house and straight for the kitchen.

Grayson followed her, eyeing the curve of her hip, his fingers aching to touch her there. But he kept to himself and waited until she got the flowers into water.

"You remembered," she said, arranging the flowers so that they were evenly spaced.

"I remember everything, Amelia." He reached out and caressed her jawline. "I would have gotten sunflowers to go with them, but the shop was fresh out."

She grinned. "Now that would've impressed me."

Pride swelled in Grayson's chest. He vividly recalled when she'd told him that her favorite flowers were daisies, followed closely by sunflowers. Then she'd said that if she ever had a garden, she was planting both so that she never had to choose. "Come on. Time for dinner."

They made small talk on the way to Woodlines. It was a fine dining establishment in downtown Keating Hollow and Amelia's favorite restaurant. When they walked in, the host immediately sat them near the front window.

"Best table in the house," Amelia said, staring out the window at the twinkling lights strewn up and down Main Street. The Valentine decorations had been removed, and now the town was glinting in white twinkle lights and bathed in moonlight. There was an elegance and charm that had won him over the first time he'd stepped foot into the valley.

Grayson reached across the table and took her hand. "Thank you for coming out with me tonight."

"Thank you for inviting me. Though considering I'm carrying your child, it feels like you're being awfully formal."

He laughed, but his mirth quickly died as he envisioned taking her to bed again. It had been months since they'd been together, and seeing her sitting across from him, her body lush and her face glowing, all he wanted to do was take her home and worship her for as long as she'd let him. But they were on their date to get to know each other in a way they hadn't before. So instead, he said, "Did you know that Hope took Levi in and gave him a place to live before they found out they were brother and sister?"

Amelia raised her eyebrows. "No. That's... amazing."

He nodded and went into details of the story about how Levi had been a homeless teen, and Hope had known firsthand what it felt like to have no one to count on and offered him a place to stay. Weeks later, they found out they shared a father. "It's astonishing how sometimes things just work out."

"Kind of like how we both ended up living in the same town," she said, eyeing him with suspicion.

Grayson laughed. "Sort of."

"Out with it. Give me the truth," she demanded, though there wasn't any anger behind her words. Just a desire for honesty, which he had to agree that she deserved. She opened her menu and studied it as she waited for his answer.

"The truth is that I took the job out here before I knew for sure you were in Keating Hollow. I needed to get out of New York for my own sanity."

"When you say before you knew for sure, does that mean you had a vision that I was out here?" she asked without looking up from her menu.

"Yes."

Her head jerked up, and she stared at him as if she hadn't expected him to answer honestly. After swallowing, she asked, "What did you see?"

Grayson twined his fingers with hers. "I saw you everywhere. The spa, the brewery, Shannon's wedding, the bookstore, and even the farmer's market. And also, the sign that leads to Keating Hollow. So while I had a good idea that you were here, I didn't know if it was permanent or that you'd taken a job with the fire department. I guess you could say that I took my job on a leap of faith that you'd be on the West Coast. You could have just been visiting for all I knew."

"Something told you that I was here though, right? The spirit witch intuition?" she asked.

He couldn't deny it and nodded.

"So it might be safe to say that you didn't exactly leave this meeting up to chance?"

Grayson laughed. "What are you getting at, Amelia?"

She put the menu down and closed it. "I wanted to be clear that this—what we have between us—isn't the universe working in mysterious ways. You missed me and deliberately found a job that meant we might have a chance. You knew I was here, and you took steps to make sure that you were, too. This reconnection isn't just something that happened to us. You manifested it."

Well, damn. When she put it like that, it wasn't as if he could deny it. She was speaking the truth. It was time to lay it all out there and make sure she understood how he felt about her and that it wasn't just about the baby. "You're right. I did do that. I regretted walking away from you, and I won't do it again."

Her lips curved into a pleased smile. "Good. Just remember

that when the baby is screaming at three in the morning and it's your turn to feed her."

Warmth spread through his chest at the idea of 3:00 a.m. feedings. A few months ago the idea would've been ludicrous. Now? He couldn't believe this was his reality.

They spent the rest of the meal talking about their new jobs, places they'd like to explore along the northern California coast, and the various residents of Keating Hollow.

"Clay and Rhys from the Keating Hollow Brewery invited me to a barbeque next week. It's out at the Townsend farm," Grayson said. "I was hoping you'd be my date."

Amelia smiled at him. "I'd love to. The Townsends are great. Yvette's the one who hooked me up with the job at the fire station. I always enjoy spending time with her."

"It's a date, then." Grayson said.

"It's a date."

They locked eyes and Grayson felt the world tilt. It was just the two of them and finally, for once, there was no question that his life was moving in the right direction. But as soon as the thought filled his mind, his phone buzzed with a text. After pulling it out of his pocket, he glanced at the notification and grimaced when he saw Kira's name flash on his screen.

"What's wrong?"

"Huh?" he asked, glancing up at Amelia, taking in her big brown eyes and worried expression. "Oh, it's nothing." He shut his phone down and shoved it in his pocket. He'd meant it when he told Kira he was done. There was no reason for her to message and even less for him to answer.

"It doesn't look like nothing," she pressed. "You look like you want to murder someone."

"Nah. I'm just annoyed a client is interrupting my date," he lied, not having any idea why he didn't just tell her it was Kira.

It was second nature to never talk about her to anyone after all the privacy issues she'd had over the years, but Grayson had already told Amelia about Kira. Or at least a version of her.

"It is late for a work call," she said. "It's not like you're a first responder." She chuckled softly. "Well, I guess some people would think it was an emergency if they ran out of their favorite wine."

Grayson laughed, relieved she wasn't pushing him about the text. If Kira kept texting, he'd find a way to tell her about it. But for now, all he wanted to do was enjoy his dinner with her.

"Hey, Grayson!" a vaguely familiar female voice called from a few tables away.

He jerked his head up and spotted Georgia Exler headed straight for them. She was an author he'd met at the Keating Hollow Brewery when he'd last been there talking to Rhys about distributing his ciders outside of town. The tall, dark-skinned woman had a warm, open face, gorgeous dark curls, and was dressed casually in a long skirt and formfitting T-shirt. "Georgia, hi," he said and then nodded to his date. "Have you met Amelia Holiday?"

Georgia gave Amelia a kind smile. "I don't think I have. You're a friend of Yvette's though, right? Fire witch?"

Amelia nodded and held her hand out to the other woman. "You must know Yvette from the bookstore."

"Yep. She's been kind enough to let me sign there a few times. Now that I'm living here in Keating Hollow, I hope to make it a regular thing."

"You're a newbie, too?" Amelia asked, her eyes lighting up. "I've only been here a couple of months."

"Yep. Just moved in last week." She studied Amelia for just a moment before she added, "Looks like we have no choice other than to be besties. Got time for coffee tomorrow at Incantation Café?"

Amelia blinked at her. "Uh, what?"

Georgia's eyes crinkled as she laughed. "We newbies need to stick together. As near as I can tell, other than Miranda, all the other women in this town have either lived here forever or are related to the Townsends. It's easier to make friends with outsiders than it is to breach that inner sanctum."

It was Amelia's turn to laugh. While she was friends with Yvette and her sisters, it was true that none of them had a lot of free time to really form new relationships. They were all newly married, getting married, or having or adopting kids. That didn't leave a lot of time for gab sessions or girls' night. "Coffee it is. Can we do it in the afternoon? I work until four."

"I'll meet you there after work," Georgia said with a smile and a nod. She turned to Grayson. "Be good to this one. I can't have you messing with my new bestie's heart."

Amelia, who'd been taking a sip of her after-dinner coffee, sputtered as she laughed.

Grayson held three fingers up in a Boy Scout salute. "You have my word."

"Good." She ruffled his hair as if she were twenty years older than him, winked at Amelia, and then strode away.

"I like her," Amelia said.

He let out a soft chuckle. "I just bet you do."

CHAPTER 11

*A*melia was on cloud nine as she walked with Grayson down Main Street. The night had been filled with good conversation, great food, and new connections. She was very excited to spend time with Georgia. Amelia made casual friends relatively easily, but she hadn't had a close friend since she lost Victoria. She missed being able to confide in someone who wasn't her brother. She loved Rex and they were close, but there were some things she just couldn't tell her brother.

"Tell me about your family," Grayson said. "Didn't you tell me you have something like nine siblings?" There was astonishment in his tone.

Normally, Amelia resented talking about her giant family. Most people were judgmental and made snarky remarks about so many mouths to feed. But knowing Grayson's history, she imagined he was curious about her life that was the polar opposite of his. "Ten actually, including Rex. But he's the only one I'm close with."

"Really? Why?" He twined his fingers with hers and guided her along the path that led to the enchanted river.

"The others are half siblings on both sides. I guess Rex and I always felt a little bit like outsiders in our own families. When your parents are having kids with their second partners and you're both shuffling back and forth, it's a strange existence. And with there being so many of us, it was easy to fade into the background, I guess. Rex and I were together most of the time and learned to lean on each other That was especially true when my dad died. He was a good man even if we weren't particularly close."

"At least you had each other," Grayson said, squeezing her hand.

Mortification shot through her and she stopped in her tracks as she realized she was complaining about being part of a huge family. Grayson hadn't had anyone. She must've sounded like a self-absorbed a-hole. "I'm sorry. You must think I'm an ungrateful jerk."

"What? No. Why would I think that?" His brows pinched together in his confusion.

"Because of what you told me. Your situation with your foster parents. You're right. I am lucky that I have Rex. And I have parents who love me. While we aren't really close, I know they're there for me if I need them."

He turned to her and wrapped his arms around her.

She stared up at him, praying he wasn't offended. "I'm sorry. That was just a stupid thing to say."

"No, it wasn't." He kissed the top of her head. "It was your truth and your reality. I don't want you to ever feel like you have to hold back just because your life wasn't as bad as mine. Gods, Amelia. I'd never want that for you. Or anyone at all. Just because you have a big family, that doesn't mean you don't have some trauma. You're a child of divorce and you've lost a parent. No matter how it turned out, it's rough on a kid when their parents break up. I get it. It must've been hard being split between two new families, always feeling like the outsiders, especially since your parents were still in the picture. It makes sense that you and Rex bonded so closely."

Amelia cupped his cheeks with both hands, feeling overwhelmed at his empathy. This was a side of him she hadn't really seen when they'd been Back East. She'd first witnessed it when he'd been helping Levi work through his issues with Silas. And now, he was validating her feelings about her childhood even though his own had been something no one should ever experience. "Thank you. I appreciate that. Just know that I was listening when you shared your past with me, and I don't ever want you to feel like I'm dismissing what you went through."

"I know." He leaned down and brushed his lips lightly over hers. When he pulled back, he said, "I had a friend who lived next door. She was my lifeline through that period. Without her, I don't know if I would've made it." He stared down at his feet as he added, "She's the only person who's ever cared about me since my parents died."

Tears filled Amelia's eyes. His admission nearly ripped her heart right out of her chest, and she wanted to wrap him in her arms and never let go. But there was one thing she needed to clear up first. With her hands squeezing his, she waited until he lifted his gaze to hers and then said, "Not the only person, Grayson. I wasn't lying when I told you I loved you back in December. It was true then, and it's true now. You're important to me and our daughter. Try to remember that, all right?"

Emotion flashed through his eyes, and he let out a breath as he tugged her to him, hugging her tightly. "I was afraid I'd messed that up."

She shook her head. "You tried, but it didn't take."

Chuckling softly, he held her for a long moment, and when he let go, he said, "You and our daughter are important to me too. More than you know."

"I think I have an idea." She grinned up at him and then tugged him down toward the river where the moon was shimmering off the water. Even though there'd been two feet of snow on the ground that morning, the town maintenance crew had already cleared the path to the river. Once she found a bench, she took a seat and gestured for him to join her.

"I heard the water has magical properties," he said as he stared at the river.

"I heard that, too." She leaned into him, loving the new closeness they were sharing. When they'd dated before, she'd fallen in love with his generosity, gentleness, and fun-loving nature, but she'd learned more about him in just a few days since they'd reunited in Keating Hollow than during the entire time they'd dated the year before. At least she'd learned more of his history and what was on the inside instead of his favorite pastry and the way he took his coffee.

He gave her a cheeky grin before turning his attention to the moonlit river again. "Didn't you tell me once that you had a golden retriever that was best friends with your shelter cat?"

Amelia couldn't help the smile that tugged at her lips. "Yes. They were inseparable. When the cat wasn't chasing the dog, they were sharing the dog bed, curling together as if they were the only two creatures in the world. It really was something."

"Sounds wonderful," he said wistfully, and she wondered if he'd ever had a pet before. But before she could ask, he stood and started waving his arms. The water rose from the river and formed in the shapes of a cat and a dog. The dog resembled a golden retriever with its floppy ears and long fluffy tail. The cat looked up at the dog and playfully swatted his nose, and when the dog shot off across the river, the cat chased after him. The two played, tormenting each other for a while, until finally the cat walked up to the dog, pressed his nose to the other beast, and then curled up next to him. The dog curled around the cat, and the image was so precious, Amelia had almost forgotten to breathe.

"It's exactly how they used to behave together." She pressed her hand to her chest. "Thank you. I miss them both so much."

"I know. The way you used to talk about them, it was clear they were special to you."

Her tears were back. He really had been paying attention to her, even when he'd been trying to hold her at arm's length. "Thank you," she said with an emotional sniff. "You're something else, you know that?"

"Nah. I'm just a spirit witch who has some strange abilities. The magic in the river is helping with this surprising skill." He conjured up the nursery, just as it was back at her house, complete with the crib and sea life mobile. "I can't wait to meet her."

Amelia clutched his arm. "Neither can I."

The scene vanished and was replaced by a dinner table with a bouquet of sunflowers and daisies, wine glasses, and what looked to be cheesecake or some sort of dessert. Musical notes floated through the air as well as heart-shaped water droplets. It was all so cheesy, and yet one of the most romantic moments Amelia had ever experienced. He hadn't just put together scenes he thought a woman would love; he'd tailored them to what he knew about her. It meant more to her than he'd ever know.

"Thank you," she whispered and then leaned in and kissed him. His lips were soft and warm in the cool night air.

Grayson caressed her cheek with his thumb as he opened

his mouth and deepened the kiss. She felt it all the way to her toes as her body started to tingle. It was exactly how she'd always felt when he touched her, only now it meant more. Now she knew he cared about her.

He pulled back, lowering his gaze as a flush colored his face. "We should probably not let that go any further."

"And why is that?" she demanded, almost offended that he'd been able to stop kissing her. Because there had been no way she was going to pry herself from his embrace. She'd missed their physical connection, and now that there was an emotional one that wasn't one-sided, she was doomed for sure.

Shifting to put distance between them, she realized that was exactly why they needed to stop. Amelia was ready for declarations and promises of forever. Grayson was just trying to navigate the shift in his existence. Sure, he obviously cared about her, but promises and forevers had been reserved for his relationship with his daughter, not Amelia. She needed to remember that, or she was in danger of getting her heart broken… again.

"Maybe we should call it a night?" she said, wrapping her arms around herself. Although it was a chilly night, it wasn't the temperature that had made her cold. It was the realization that she was likely getting ahead of herself again. There was a reason she'd already told him they needed to give this relationship time to grow. Pushing for more would only backfire. She was sure of that.

"Yeah, I guess we should." He pulled her to his side, giving her a sideways hug and kissing her temple. "I had a really good time with you tonight."

"Same here." They walked hand in hand back to Main Street and to his SUV. Once she was tucked into the passenger seat and he was driving them back toward her house, Amelia said, "Tell me more about your neighbor. The one who was there for you as a kid. Did you stay in touch?"

His expression was hidden in the shadows, but she could have sworn she saw him stiffen at her questions.

"You don't have to answer," she rushed out. "If you don't want to talk about that time, I understand."

"No, it's not that," he said gruffly. "I was just caught off guard." There was silence for a moment before he continued. "The first few years at that foster home were truly unbearable. There was no effort to make sure I had the counseling I needed after the accident. I was expected to be the model child. Quiet, obedient, and most of all, unemotional. They had taken me in, so I was to be grateful or they'd send me back. Few fates are worse than the state group home where kids wait to find a forever family, so I did what they wanted. But I was numb inside. I'd lost a world I loved and got an emotional prison instead."

Amelia's heart ached, and she desperately wished she hadn't asked any questions. This wasn't how she wanted to end their lovely evening. "I'm so sorry, Grayson. I had no idea."

"No one does," he said simply. "Not even Kira."

"Kira?" she asked, frowning. "The model you dated for a while?"

This time she felt it when he flinched, but she didn't comment on it. He was talking about his past, something she knew he never did and suspected he really needed to do. "Yes," he said. "Kira was my neighbor. We also dated for a short time but realized pretty quickly that we should just be friends."

"That makes sense," Amelia said. "She's your childhood friend, the one you leaned on through everything. Messing it up with a romantic relationship would be scary."

He glanced at her for a moment, his brows drawn together

as if he was contemplating what she'd just said. But then he shook his head. "We weren't on the same page. That's all. We did remain friends, but we're not as close as we used to be. We were there for each other as kids, and for that, I'll be forever grateful. But now? I'll always love her because of that shared history, though we've both chosen two different paths and now our friendship doesn't make as much sense."

"I think it's a little sad that your friendship has changed, but there are some people who move into your life for a certain time and then drift out again. It's okay to see it like that."

He nodded. "Yes. I think that's right. She saved me when I needed her most, and I saved her when she needed me most. That's enough, right?"

"Sure." She reached over and squeezed his leg lightly. "There aren't any rules for how to navigate your relationships, Grayson. All you can do is keep an open heart."

He pulled into her driveway and walked her to her door. "Just so you know... my heart is open to you."

She smiled up at him. "That's good."

Grayson pulled her to him, pressing his large body against hers as he kissed her lightly.

Amelia nearly melted under his touch, but then came alive as he deepened the kiss and made her head swim. When he finally stepped back, she was breathless and moments from throwing her rules out the window and inviting him in. She'd told herself they needed time to really get to know each other this time before she invited him back into her bed. But what did that matter when he made her feel so good?

"Good night, Amelia," he said, already retreating from the porch.

"You're not staying?" she blurted, and then she immediately regretted it when his eyes crinkled at the edges.

"Not tonight, love. Get some sleep. I'll call you tomorrow."

Amelia let herself into her empty house and watched from the front window as his taillights disappeared down the hill.

CHAPTER 12

*G*rayson groaned as he drove down the mountain back into town. Amelia had wanted him to stay, and what had he done? He'd decided to embrace his chivalrous side and declined. What was wrong with him? He could've followed her into the house. That didn't mean he had to spend the night, right?

Wrong.

That kiss they'd shared would've escalated quickly. He knew where they were headed, and their relationship was too important to him to rush it. It wouldn't kill him to wait it out, to spend more time getting closer to her before they fell into bed together.

But damn, did he want her. He missed spending time in her bed. The problem was that their relationship had centered on the physical side previously, and he wanted more than that now. She was worth the wait.

When Grayson pulled his Toyota into his driveway, he noted the light in the front window and frowned. He didn't remember leaving any lights other than the porch light on when he'd left earlier. He wasn't one for using extra energy. Deciding he must've accidentally flipped a switch on his way out, he didn't think much of it as he let himself into his house.

He'd just dropped his keys into a bowl on the small table near the front door when he heard a familiar voice say, "It's about time you got here."

A chill ran down his spine as he turned and stared at the woman who'd somehow found a way to let herself into his home. His oldest friend, Kira, the woman known to the world as Katy Carmichael, was lounging in an oversized chair, holding a mug. "Kira, what the hell are you doing here? And how did you get into my house?"

She uncurled like a cat and got to her feet, her six-inch heels making her just an inch shorter than his six feet. "You didn't answer any of my texts or phone calls, Grayson. What else did you expect me to do?"

"Not break into my house?" he fumed. The scent of fresh coffee was in the air, and he marveled at her ability to just make herself right at home. He stalked into his kitchen to find that the dishes he'd left in the sink earlier had been put in the dishwasher and there was a bouquet of fresh flowers on his table. "What the hell is this? Did you think cleaning up and bringing me flowers would keep me from being angry?"

"Please. You're not upset that I broke in. You're just upset that I'm here," she countered as she followed him.

He grabbed a glass and filled it with water from the tap. Without saying a word, he downed the cool liquid, wishing it was something stronger. But he didn't keep alcohol in his house anymore. Not after what had happened in New York a few months ago.

Grayson met her icy blue gaze. Seeing her outside of her posh New York City apartment, it occurred to him that he couldn't see any traces of the girl he'd dated those few years right out of high school. Kira Jamison had been completely consumed by Katy Carmichael. The pretty brunette with the intelligent blue eyes and soft curves had been replaced by a platinum blonde, with a cool gaze and a too-thin body. The first time she hadn't fit into a sample size, she'd gone on a starvation diet and didn't let up until she resembled a runway model.

Kira moved so that she was standing behind him. She placed her hand on his hip and whispered in his ear, "Come on, Grayson. You can't stay mad at me." She moved her hand so that it was flat against his stomach, her pinky touching the button of his jeans. "I've missed you. I thought maybe we could put everything behind us and try again. I'm always better when we're together."

He placed his hand over hers and removed it. "What are you doing?"

"Just trying to show my interest," she said flippantly as she took a step back. "No need to get testy about it."

"Did you seriously just imply that you wanted to have sex with me?" he blurted as he turned to face her.

She laughed, her eyes full of amusement. "Would that be so shocking? It's not like we haven't done it before."

He shook his head, dumbfounded as he placed his water glass on the counter and said, "Cut the shit, Kira. We haven't had that kind of relationship in years. Don't act like anything has changed just because you brought me some flowers. Now, tell me why you're really here."

"I was just messing with you. Chill out, okay?" Her smile vanished as her expression changed to one of pure irritation. "I told you. I'm here because you didn't answer my calls."

"You just started texting today," he said, furrowing his

brow. "Are you trying to tell me that you were so worried when I didn't pick up right away that you flew all the way from New York to California? Because I have to say, that sounds crazy even for you."

She huffed out a breath of irritation. "Of course not. I was already on my way. I figured you'd answer before I got here. When you didn't, I made myself at home. Just as I'd expect you to do if you came to see me. Are you really pissed that I had Benji pick a lock for me?"

Grayson was listening to her, but nothing was making sense. She'd been on her way to Keating Hollow? Benji, her driver, had apparently picked his lock and then left since there wasn't another car parked in his driveway. Instead of trying to guess what she was up to, he grabbed his glass and refilled it then said, "I think we'd better go sit down."

"Whatever you say." She quickly topped off her mug with more coffee and then followed him into the other room.

He sat on the couch, placed his drink on the coffee table, and leaned forward, resting his elbows on his knees. Kira took her spot on the oversized chair, but instead of sprawling all over it again, she sat with her back straight and her mug cupped in both hands.

The change in the way she carried herself got his attention. Her self-confidence was gone, and she looked very unsure of herself. He hadn't seen her like that since they were both teenagers. Certainly not since she'd become known as Katy Carmichael. Her entire persona was built around never showing weakness. Not even to him. It was ultimately what had doomed them as a couple.

When he'd first realized she was there, he'd assumed she'd come to Keating Hollow to try to entice him back to New York and to get him to work for her again. He'd been on her payroll, cleaning up her messes, for many years, but after what happened in December, he'd informed her he was leaving and wouldn't be back. She hadn't been happy about it, but to his surprise, she'd let him go. He'd naively believed that she'd respect his wishes and let him live his life in peace. He peered at her, unsettled by her demeanor. Something was wrong. Something more than the rift in their friendship. No matter how frustrated he was with her, she was still important to him, and he knew he wouldn't let her go until he found out the true reason for her visit. "What is it?"

"I think I need to make some changes in my life," she said.

That seemed fairly obvious. There was a reason he'd walked out of her life. "Okay."

She bit her lower lip and glanced away, unable to look him in the eye. Whatever was bothering her, it was going to take her a minute to get it out. He sat back on his couch and waited.

"I've been doing a lot of thinking since you left," she said. "And you're right. My life is a mess. I think I need to take a step back from acting for a bit and reassess what's most important."

He blinked at her, completely taken aback. Just a couple of months ago, she'd told him in no uncertain terms that she was living the life of her dreams and she didn't appreciate his judgment. It had been the morning after one of her friends had almost died of a drug overdose and no one had wanted to take her to the hospital. They'd insisted she just needed to sleep it off. Of course, they'd all been so drunk or high they could barely walk, much less discern if their friend needed medical attention.

Disgusted, Grayson had taken her to the hospital over their objections. By the next morning, when it was clear she would've died if he hadn't intervened, he'd made the decision that he couldn't be in Kira's world anymore. He could put up with a lot, but her out-of-control partying and inability to take responsibility for anything was more than he could handle. He'd been hoping she'd grow out of her party days, but it had started to feel like he'd be waiting forever. "What do you mean by reassess?"

"That thing that happened with Heather... I keep having nightmares about it." Her voice cracked, and a tear fell unchecked down her cheek. Her eyes were glassy as she met his gaze, and pain was reflected back at him. Suddenly Katy Carmichael was gone, replaced by that young girl he'd grown up with.

His breath caught as he realized that his Kira was still in there somewhere. The girl he'd loved with all his heart wasn't completely lost. "Heather's okay, though, right?"

She nodded and sniffed. "She checked herself into a rehab center a week ago. She asked me to take her, but I refused because I didn't want the paparazzi catching me at a place like that. She called me selfish and told me that I deserved for you to leave me." Her voice was barely audible as she added, "She said that I didn't care about anyone but myself."

They were the same words he'd said to her when he walked out for the last time. He wanted to comfort her, to tell her there was still time to change, to become the person she wanted to be, but he didn't. He'd said words like that too many times to count, and each time she'd ignored him.

Grayson sat in silence, because if he'd learned anything about Katy Carmichael, it was that she didn't respond to platitudes. She had a stubborn streak a mile long, and that trait had served her well when it came to the acting business. On the personal level, it had been detrimental. Grayson couldn't save her. Only she could do that. He decided not to comment on Heather's remarks. Instead, he focused on trying to help

Kira. "Maybe you should speak to a professional if you keep having the nightmares."

She nodded. "I already am. She told me the first thing I had to do was forgive myself."

"Have you?"

She shook her head. "No. You were right. I *am* a horrible person."

He winced. Had he said that to her face? Probably. He'd been beyond angry the last time they'd spoken. "You were horrible in that moment, but that's not the entirety of you," he said, meaning it. She was, after all, still the girl who'd been there for him after he'd left his foster parent's house, and she had held his hand when he'd finally gone to visit his parents' graves for the first time. "But we both know I can't absolve you of your guilt. If that's what you're looking for, then—"

"It's not," she said urgently. "I just needed to get away from everything."

"So you came here? To Keating Hollow? Why not your beach house on the Cape or your mountain cabin in Vail?"

She squeezed her eyes shut and shook her head. When she opened them again, she held his gaze, and with raw emotion in her voice, she said, "It wouldn't do me any good to go to either of those places. I need to escape the people in my circles. But more than that, I need you. You're the only one who can center me. Do you think I can stay for a few days? I need a place where no one will find me."

Why was it up to him to center her? He was starting a new life in Keating Hollow. One that was far removed from her world. Grayson wanted to tell her to stay at the inn, but he gritted his teeth, knowing he couldn't. Since Silas Ansell had moved to Keating Hollow, there were a handful of paparazzi that hung around. They'd see her for sure, and whatever soul-searching retreat she was on would be ruined. Reluctantly, he nodded his head. "Yes, but this doesn't change anything. I won't be coming back to New York."

She sighed. "I wish I could change your mind about that."

"I know. But you won't. Amelia Holiday is here, and she's pregnant with my child." He hadn't meant to blurt out his news like that, but it had to be said. She'd know better than anyone what a child meant to him.

Her eyes widened, and then the color drained out of her face.

"You look like you're going to pass out," he said, watching her closely.

She sucked in a sharp breath and pressed a hand to her chest. "Is that why you left me?"

He shook his head. "No. You know why I left. I just found out a few days ago about the baby. And before you ask, yes, Amelia and I are dating again."

"That's..." She cleared her throat. "That's really wonderful, Grayson. I know how much having a family means to you."

He just nodded, because it wasn't a conversation he wanted to have with her.

"Do you love her?"

Grayson stood, not answering her. "Come on. I'll show you to the guest room."

She sighed, seeming to understand that she'd overstepped. After grabbing a suitcase that was sitting in the corner near the front door, she followed him down the hall and didn't utter a word when he opened the door to the small room with a double bed.

The accommodations were modest at best, and the fact that she didn't complain even once as she tucked her suitcase into the closet surprised him. He expected Katy to appear and act the princess like she usually did when things weren't up to her standards. But when she didn't, he stared down at her, believing for the first time since she'd arrived that she might actually be serious about making a change.

"Thanks, Grayson." She leaned in, kissing him on the cheek. Then she patted him on the shoulder and said, "Now go on. I need to get my beauty rest."

He pulled her into a hug, holding on for a moment longer than necessary, and said, "I missed you."

She let out a little sob and clutched him tighter as she forced out, "Me, too."

CHAPTER 13

"*A*melia!" Georgia called from her table near a window in Incantation Café. Her tight curls were pulled up into a ponytail, and she looked like someone out of a gothic movie with her leggings, lace up boots, and flowing violet lace top.

"You look gorgeous," Amelia said, suddenly feeling self-conscious about her jeans and sweatshirt. It had been a quiet day at the fire station, and she'd spent her time updating the procedures manual. Her eyes were tired from staring at the computer, but she was more than ready for some human interaction.

"Thanks." Georgia chuckled. "I don't get out much, so when I have a reason to leave the house, I try to make the most of it. Mind telling me where you got those jeans? They do great things for your backside."

Amelia felt a smile tug at her lips. "This great boutique back home in New York. I'll get you the website if you want."

"Yes, please."

"Okay. I'll have to look it up, but I'll text it to you. Now, why don't you leave the house much?" Amelia asked as she took a seat across from her new friend.

"I write from home." She shrugged. "When I'm on deadline, I don't emerge for anything other than take out. I can get a little feral." She grinned and took a sip of her coffee.

"I'll have to pick up a book of yours. I thought Yvette said she keeps signed copies at her store. Is she stocking yours?"

"Yep. They are right next to Miranda's. The two resident writers have special privileges. But enough about that. Tell me about you and that gorgeous date of yours last night."

Amelia felt her cheeks flush as she thought of Grayson and that kiss they'd shared the night before. In fact, she hadn't stopped thinking about it since he dropped her off. If she'd had her way, he'd have stayed over, and now she was wondering how long he was going to make her wait. After all, it had been months since they'd been together. "Grayson and I... Well, we used to date when we lived Back East. When it ended, I came out here. And much to my surprise, he followed. So we're seeing how things go."

"Oh, intrigue. I can't wait to find out why things ended the first time." Georgia rubbed her hands together as if there was some great scandal to uncover.

The truth was Amelia also wanted to know why it ended. She had thought he'd run because she confessed her feelings to him. But now she wasn't so sure. He had taken the news of the baby in stride and seemed all in with whatever was to come next. Had there been another reason? He'd started opening up to her, but there was no doubt he still had secrets. "I guess you'll just have to wait until Miranda and Cameron turn our story into a movie."

Georgia threw her head back and laughed. "Oh, I like you. We're going to be great friends."

"I hope I can get in on that action," Hanna Pelsh said, smiling as she sat in one of the chairs next to Georgia. "A girl can never have enough friends. Especially when all her current ones are starting families. Did you hear Yvette's news?"

Amelia shook her head. She'd been holed up in a snowstorm after all.

"No, do tell," Georgia said, leaning forward as if waiting for a juicy secret.

"She and Jacob are on their way to the Bay Area to pick up the baby they are adopting. They just found out last night. Isn't that exciting?"

"Oh, wow," Georgia said. "I knew they had started the process, but I had no idea it would happen so soon. She's going to have her hands full, isn't she?"

"Yep. With Skye running around and the new baby, I fear it's going to be pandemonium at their house. They'll both love it."

Amelia unconsciously pressed a hand to her stomach as she grinned at the pretty café owner. They'd become friendly over the past few months since Amelia was nearly a daily visitor either before or after work. "You look like you're looking forward to being an auntie again."

Hanna chuckled. She'd grown up with the Townsends and was best friends with Faith, who owned the town spa and had recently moved into a new house she and her husband built. "Yes, the Townsend sisters are on a roll. Abby's due in August, Noel's youngest isn't even a year old yet, and Yvette will soon have a newborn. That leaves Faith, who hasn't made it a secret that she and Hunter are trying, and Hope, who is applying to be a foster parent. It's a lot. Meanwhile, Rhys and I aren't in any hurry. I think we'll try a dog first. Maybe."

They all laughed. Then Georgia said, "Well, you can count on me. No kids here and no plans to make or acquire any."

They both looked at Amelia.

She cleared her throat. "Can't say the same." She glanced down at the barely there baby bump. "My little one is due in July. But I'm good for girls' night any time. One last hurrah, right?"

Georgia and Hanna both let out surprised cries and then congratulated her.

"It looks like you settled in the right town," Hanna said. "There will be no shortage of playdates and other moms to bond with."

Amelia swallowed hard. There was no doubt that she wanted her child with every fiber of her being, but the realities of actually being a mother hadn't hit her until that very moment.

"Uh-oh," Georgia said, reaching out and grabbing her hand. "Take a breath. Are you dizzy?"

Was she? Yes, she believed she was. Nodding, she pressed a hand to her spinning head, hoping to make it stop.

"Here. Eat this," an unfamiliar woman said.

Amelia eyed the coffee cake and took it without question. After a few bites the spinning stopped, and she no longer felt as if she'd faint straight away. "Thank you," she said, looking up at the platinum blonde standing near their table.

Hanna and Georgia were gaping at her, appearing to be speechless.

"You're very welcome. You're Amelia Holiday, aren't you?"

"Yes." Amelia frowned, trying to place the woman. She looked so familiar, but Amelia had no recollection of who she was. "I'm sorry. Have we met before?"

The woman laughed. "No, we haven't. But I've been looking

forward to getting to know you. I'm Katy Carmichael, Grayson's oldest and dearest friend."

Amelia was stunned speechless as she stared up at pure perfection. No wonder she was familiar. The woman had been in three hit movies over the past couple years and had starred in a long-running television series that ended a few years before. "Katy Carmichael. I, um, you said you're friends with Grayson?"

The woman smiled kindly down at her. "Best friends. I'm sorry to intrude. After Grayson and I talked last night, I just couldn't wait to meet you." She turned to Hanna and said, "Can you bring Amelia another coffee cake and something to drink? We don't want her blood sugar to drop again."

"Oh, gosh. Of course. I actually came over here to take her order and we got caught up chatting." She turned to Amelia. "I'm so sorry about that. Coffee cake and a decaf mocha, extra whip?"

"Sure," Amelia said, still trying to make sense of what Katy had said. They'd spoken last night? Katy was his oldest friend? Hadn't he mentioned that Katy was acquainted with his friend Kira who'd lived next door to him? "Thanks, Hanna."

"Of course." Hanna hurried back to the counter while Georgia held her hand out to Katy and gushed over how much she'd loved her last movie. Katy was polite but steered the conversation back to Amelia quickly.

"Since it looks like we're going to be spending a lot of time together, we should probably have dinner to get to know each other better," Katy said to Amelia.

"We are?" Amelia asked, feeling stupid and about ten steps behind in the conversation. She'd been caught completely off guard and had no idea how a literal movie star had ended up sitting with her and Georgia in Incantation Café. Other than Silas, Keating Hollow wasn't known for attracting celebrities.

"Of course. Since I'm living with Grayson, I assume we'll see each other all the time."

Hanna returned and placed the drink and coffee cake on the table. "Here you go."

Amelia was too busy gaping at Katy to answer Hanna. "You're... um, *living* with Grayson?"

Katy chuckled. "Yep. I needed a break from the industry, so I came here to Grayson's. But don't worry. We've lived with each other off and on for years. In fact, ever since he moved out a couple months ago, I've been missing waking up next to him. The man is a human furnace. But I'm guessing you already know that."

Amelia's stomach rolled. "You sleep in the same bed?"

"Sometimes. Usually after we've been drinking. You know how it is when alcohol is involved." Katy stood. "Anyway, I need to get going. I'm meeting Grayson at the brewery. Are you free tomorrow for dinner? My treat."

No. Say no, Amelia told herself. She wasn't sure she could survive a dinner alone with the actress if she had to hear about her sleeping in the same bed with Grayson. "I'm not sure I'm free," Amelia hedged.

"Oh, come on. I'll tell you all about the time Grayson and I nearly got arrested as we were leaving Amsterdam." Katy flashed a million-dollar smile and added, "He's such a good guy. I'm really thrilled that he found someone he cares so much about."

"Yeah, okay," Amelia found herself saying. There couldn't be anything going on between them. Not after that last statement. It was clear Katy knew she and Grayson were seeing each other. Maybe she really did just want to make friends. But that didn't explain why Katy was living with him or the fact that Grayson hadn't mentioned it even once.

"Great! How about we meet at the Cozy Cave at six? There's an ahi tuna dish on the menu that looks incredible," Katy said. "Then we can both spill all the dirt on our favorite person."

"Okay," Amelia said again, feeling like she'd just been railroaded. Katy had swept in like a hurricane, dropped some concerning news, and managed to convince her it was a good idea to spend time together all in the span of about five minutes.

"It's a date." Katy stood, winked at Amelia, waved at Hanna and Georgia, and then disappeared as quickly as she'd arrived.

The three of them stared after her. When the door closed behind her, Georgia said, "Holy witch's brew. Did that really just happen?"

"That was... crazy," Hanna added.

Amelia blinked at both of them. Finally, she cleared her throat and asked, "Did you guys get the feeling that Katy Carmichael is major trouble with a capital T? And not in the good way?"

"Definitely," Georgia said. "That sickeningly fake niceness combined with expert-level manipulation is perfect for the villain in my next book."

"You need to be careful with that one," Hanna said thoughtfully, still staring at the door where the other woman had disappeared. "If it's true she and Grayson are longtime friends, it's going to be hard to shake her if she is up to something shady. You don't want him to have to take sides."

"Especially if you don't know which side he'd land on," Georgia said.

Amelia groaned. "That's what I was afraid of."

They both gave her sympathetic looks. Georgia reached across the table and covered one of Amelia's hands with hers. Hanna did the same. Georgia squeezed and said, "Just remember that we're here if you need to talk. Heck, we're here if you just want a margarita." She grinned at Amelia. "And no matter what goes down, we're on your side. Just try not to get us in a situation where we need to bury the body."

Hanna laughed, her eyes twinkling with mirth. Georgia just shrugged one shoulder and cracked a smile. "Yeah, digging graves isn't really my thing. So do your best, okay?" Hanna added.

Amelia shook her head, chuckling at them. But then she beamed and squeezed both of their hands as she said, "Thank you. When's margarita night? I'll bring the mocktails."

"Shoot. Pregnant lady in the house," Georgia said, lightly slapping her forehead with her palm. "Appetizers then."

"I'm still having a margarita," Hanna said, waving at someone who'd walked into the café.

"And I'll be sipping the virgin kind." Amelia picked up the coffee cake and took a big bite. Once she swallowed, she added, "Or I'll just eat this. Damn, Hanna. What do you put in these?"

"You know. The usual," Hanna said. "Let's do margarita night Saturday. By then you'll have a ton of good gossip for us. I mean, since you'll be hobnobbing with a literal movie star."

"I'm in," Georgia said.

"Saturday it is," Amelia said with a sigh. "Let's just hope I make it that long without killing anyone."

Georgia stood and clasped a hand on Amelia's shoulder. "I have faith."

Hanna agreed.

Amelia just shook her head and said, "You two are enjoying this entirely too much."

"That's what friends are for," Georgia said. "We're there for the highs and lows and everything in between. I know we just met, but I can sense that we're going to be great friends. Now go. Get out of here and get yourself some real food. Gotta keep that baby fed."

With happy tears in her eyes, Amelia gave them both a quick hug, promised to let them know if anything really juicy happened, and then walked out of the café, already calling Grayson.

CHAPTER 14

*G*rayson clutched the wheel of his Toyota as he navigated the winding mountain highway. His day had been spent on the northern most point of the California coast, talking to various restaurant owners and buyers. He was determined to help the Keating Hollow Brewery distribute their ciders up and down the 101 corridor. The ciders were popular, and this was the push they needed to expand production.

He'd risen early, did his best to dodge Kira, and then had taken off, determined to get the job done in time to make his appointment with Rhys, the man who was the genius behind the Keating Hollow Brewery ciders. He needed to nail down contracts so that the brewery knew just how much they needed to put into the expansion to meet demand. Normally he didn't take such a big interest in their suppliers, but he'd connected with Rhys the first night he'd been in Keating Hollow and really believed in their product.

And if he was being honest with himself, it felt good using

his talents of persuasion for something good instead of keeping spoiled stars out of trouble.

Once Grayson emerged from the mountain and took a right onto the highway that led back into Keating Hollow, his phone chimed with notifications of a mix of texts and phone calls. He groaned. Kira had been trying to get him on the phone for most of the day, but he'd let all the calls go to voicemail and sent her a text that he was busy with clients. It appeared her patience had run out.

Too bad, he thought, because he still had one more appointment to make before he called it a day.

His phone rang again, but this time it wasn't Kira. Amelia's name flashed on the screen mounted in his dash. He pressed the button to answer it and spoke over the Bluetooth system. "Amelia, how was your day?"

"I guess I'd describe it as *interesting*." There was no mistaking the irritation in her tone.

"What happened?" he asked, pressing his foot on the accelerator. The sooner he got to town, the sooner he could run up to Amelia's house and… do what? He wasn't sure, but he ached to spend a quiet evening with her instead of dealing with whatever Kira wanted.

"I met your bestie today."

"Huh?"

"Katy Carmichael? She said you've lived together off and on for years and that she misses waking up next to you," Amelia said.

"What the hell?" Adrenaline shot through Grayson, and he had to force himself to not put the pedal to the floor. Getting into a car accident before he could ring Kira's neck wasn't acceptable. "Kira came to see you?"

"Kira? No. Katy. The actress. She said you two have been friends for years. She ambushed me at Incantation Café."

"Dammit. I'm sorry, Amelia. Kira is Katy's given name. She changed it for her acting career. I'd really rather talk to you about this in person. Where are you? Your house? I can be there in fifteen minutes."

"No. I'm not home. And honestly, Grayson, I don't really want to talk to you right now. I have some processing to do. Besides, I hear you have a date. Far be it from me to cause trouble. Just go have a good evening. I'll talk to you in a day or two."

"I don't have a date. Where'd you get that idea?" he asked, though he could guess if Kira had been involved.

No response.

"Amelia?"

Silence.

"Dammit." He hit the End button and told the car to call Amelia. It immediately went to voicemail. "Amelia, I just need to let you know that Kira showed up last night. I had no idea she was coming here, and I haven't even talked to her since I left New York. I'm sorry she ambushed you. Please call me back."

He ended the call and thumped the steering wheel with his palm in frustration. What was wrong with Kira? The night before she'd seemed vulnerable and ready to change. But what he'd just heard from Amelia told him that had all been a lie. She had to know that he wouldn't like her tormenting Amelia. And what about the paparazzi? Surely they were bound to get wind of her. Their lives were about to be splattered on the front page of all the gossip rags.

Grayson gritted his teeth and tried to ignore the throbbing right above his left eye. This was the kind of shit he'd hoped to never have to deal with again. He should've known he'd never be free of it.

As he rolled into town, he contemplated heading straight for Amelia's house but knew he needed to give her space. She'd said she didn't want to talk, and since she hadn't called him back, he had to honor that.

One thing he knew he *wasn't* going to do was go home where Kira was surely waiting for him. No, he was going to keep his appointment with Rhys and hope that Amelia would be ready to talk soon. He needed to explain, and he desperately wanted to know what else Kira had told her.

The parking lot at the Keating Hollow Brewery was still full for the evening when he pulled into the last available spot. Glancing at the clock, he frowned. It was getting close to eight, kind of late for a full house. He decided that they were likely holding an event and hoped Rhys wouldn't be too busy to meet with him.

There was a lot of chatter when he tugged the door open, but there wasn't any live entertainment, nor did there appear to be an organized event. Grayson nodded to the hostess and pointed to the bar.

She smiled at him and returned his nod as she leaned down to talk to another customer she'd just seated.

The bar was crowded, but he found a seat at the very end where Lin Townsend usually sat and hopped up on the stool. Both Rhys and Clay, the manager, were behind the counter pouring beers and ciders from the taps.

Rhys spotted him and raised a finger, indicating he'd be with him in a moment.

Grayson called, "Take your time." Then he turned around and scanned the brewery. It took only a few seconds for him to realize why there was such a large crowd.

Katy Carmichael was holding court at a table in the back that wasn't visible from the entrance. She was sitting on the table itself, signing autographs and preening for selfies.

Holy freakin' attention whore. What had gotten into her? Had she lost her mind? She was going to be all over the front page of every gossip rag from Hollywood to London.

"Grayson!" she called, waving at him, her smile so bright he thought it might blind him.

He was careful not to scowl at her. No doubt someone would snap that picture and then there'd be an even bigger PR nightmare. Grayson had been wary to never make the story about him when they were spotted in public together. Just once, right after they'd broken up, one of the photographers had heard them arguing. And the very next day, Grayson's picture, along with his life story, had been up for public consumption. It had been one of the worst weeks of his life, seeing the pictures in a few of the magazines of the car crash that had taken his parents from him.

Thankfully, Grayson was no one in the entertainment industry, and his part in the story had faded away quickly when Kira started seeing an actor whose star was on the rise.

"What took you so long?" Kira asked, slipping her arm around his waist and peering up at him with adoring eyes. He knew that look. It was the one that meant she was playing this up for the audience, even if that audience only included the residents of Keating Hollow. "I was starting to think you'd stood me up."

Grayson leaned down and whispered in her ear, "It's hard to stand someone up when you haven't made a date."

She blinked up at him, her blue eyes wide. "I disagree. This morning I asked where we were having dinner tonight. You said the Keating Hollow Brewery, and I said, 'Great. I'll meet you there.'"

He frowned, recalling that the conversation had been very different. She'd asked when he'd be back, and he'd said he didn't know because he had an appointment at the brewery. She'd said something about picking up burgers, and he'd nodded. That was not a plan to eat out together. "I have a business meeting, Kira," he said through clenched teeth, annoyed he had to deal with this at all.

"Of course. You go ahead. I'll be right here when you're done." She gave him a brilliant smile and floated back to the table and her adoring fans.

Grayson took a deep breath and turned away from her, willing himself to put her out of his mind. He had business to attend to. If Kira wanted to blow up her quiet existence in Keating Hollow that was on her. She knew better. He didn't need to babysit her anymore.

"Grayson, hey, man," Rhys said, holding his hand out. "It's kind of crazy in here tonight." He nodded toward Katy Carmichael and chuckled. "I swear, who would've thought Keating Hollow would become the go-to spot for some of today's hottest celebs?"

"It does seem surreal, doesn't it?" Grayson said, forcing a smile. "Good for business though."

"Definitely. Come on back to the office so we can talk shop." Rhys waved him behind the counter, and Grayson was relieved to leave the celebrity spectacle behind him.

"I have good news," Grayson said when he sat across from Rhys in the orderly office. "I've secured another half dozen accounts between here and Smith River. They aren't huge, but there are a couple in Crescent City that are popular places for the locals that should prove promising. I have the initial orders here." He pulled out his laptop and opened a spreadsheet. "I think these, along with the contracts I've already secured, should be sufficient for my company to win exclusive distribution of the territory as well as to guarantee enough orders that you should be able to expand production."

"This looks really promising, Grayson," Rhys said, peering at the spreadsheet. "Let's go over terms."

The two men spent the next ten minutes going over their contract and then another hour about the brewery's expansion plans. By the time they emerged from the office, Grayson had completely forgotten about Kira and her antics. But as soon as they found their way back into the dining room, he spotted her sitting at the bar and trying to flirt with Clay. She had her hand on his arm, smiling prettily up at him the way she did when she wanted something from someone.

"It was a pleasure, Rhys. Thanks for taking time out of your evening to meet with me."

Rhys chuckled and shook Grayson's hand with both of his. "I should be the one thanking you. Clay and Lin are going to be really pleased by this development. You've done right by us."

Pride filled Grayson, solidifying that he'd made the right choice when he left New York. He enjoyed working with the small breweries and wineries around the area, doing his part to help the family-run small businesses. "It's just good business," he said, smiling back at Rhys. "I know a good product when I taste it."

"Good man." Rhys thumped him on the back and disappeared back into the office.

Grayson steeled himself and went to save Clay.

"Katy," Grayson said from right behind her. "Are you ready to go?"

She spun, and her eyes lit up when she spotted him. There'd

been a time when he would've done anything to see that look on her face. Now he felt... indifferent. "Wait, we need to get dinner."

"I'm not all that hungry. I had a late lunch," he lied. "If you want a ride, I'm headed home." It occurred to him he had no idea how she'd gotten to town, and he didn't really care at that point. His head was aching, and he still needed to try to patch things up with Amelia.

"You're no fun," she said as she followed him out the door.

"Neither are you," he muttered and climbed into his SUV, not bothering to open her door for her.

She let out an irritated huff and climbed in. "What is your problem? Is it really so awful to have dinner with your best friend?"

He glared at her. "What did you say to Amelia? And why in the hell did you seek her out at all?"

She jerked back and blinked at him in feigned surprise. He was willing to bet most people wouldn't have realized she was acting, but he'd known her for a very long time, and the Kira that was in his SUV at that moment was not *his* Kira. This one was putting on an act, and he had no idea why. "I just happened to run into her at the café, so I said hi. What's so wrong with that?"

"I don't know. You tell me. She certainly didn't seem too thrilled to learn that we had a *date* tonight."

"Oh, for the love of the gods." She threw up her hands. "I was just being friendly and mentioned that we were meeting for dinner tonight. Friends still have dinner, right? It's not my fault she got jealous."

Grayson side-eyed her. "You think she was jealous?"

She shrugged. "Probably."

"You do realize we didn't have plans for dinner, right?"

Kira rolled her eyes. "Do we have to go over this again?"

"Nope. But I would like to know what's going on with you. Last night you seemed as if you wanted a place to hang out away from the spotlight. And now today, you were running around town and holding court at the brewery. As soon as those selfies hit social media, your whereabouts are going to go viral. Was it really too hard to lay low for twenty-four hours?"

"That's not—" She shook her head and crossed her arms over her chest, staring out the window.

"That's not what?" Grayson turned onto his street and a moment later, he pulled into the driveway. The house was dark; not even the porch light was on.

"Forget it." She jumped out of the vehicle and stomped up to the front door where she produced a key and let herself in.

He followed her inside and raised an eyebrow, wondering where she'd found the key. He knew he had a spare but had no idea where he'd left it.

"There's something wrong. Your dramatic mood shift from last night to today is too theatrical, even for you. I think you'd better just tell me what's really going on," Grayson said, already knowing he was going to regret his next words. "If it's going to hit the press, it's better if you tell me now. I might be able to mitigate the damage."

"It's nothing like that," she said as she flopped down on the couch. "It has to do with my mother."

Grayson sank into his chair and waited for the rest. She didn't have the closest relationship with her parents, but they usually managed to get along okay. "What happened?"

She stared at her hands that were clasped in her lap. "She doesn't—"

"Sweet Child O' Mine" started playing on Grayson's phone, cutting her off. It was Amelia's ringtone, and he immediately put his finger up, indicating he had to take the call. "Amelia?" he said into the phone. "Thanks for—"

"Levi is taking me to the healer," she blurted. "Something's wrong with the baby."

Grayson's blood ran cold, and his hands started to shake. "What is it?"

"I don't know. I have some back pain and some bleeding." Her voice trembled, and he knew that she was crying.

"I'll be right there. It's going to be fine, I promise," he said, not having any idea if that was true. "Hang in there, okay? I'm on my way." Grayson grabbed his jacket and keys, and right before he ran out the door, he glanced back at Kira. "It's the baby. I have to go."

Shock registered on her face as she nodded and whispered, "Go. They need you."

He swallowed hard and left Kira and her explanation behind as he raced to the healers' office on Main Street.

CHAPTER 15

*A*melia was on the verge of hysterics by the time Levi pulled to a stop in front of the healers' office.

Gerry Whipple strode out of the office, her expression stern as she pulled the car door open. Her husband, Martin, followed her with a wheelchair.

"How are things now, Amelia?" she asked as she gently helped Amelia from the truck.

"I'm scared," she said, holding her belly as she winced at the movement. "Is my baby going to be all right?"

"First we're going to take a look, and then we'll do everything we can to ensure you and the baby are safe. Now, sit in that chair and let Martin wheel you in. I'll only be a minute."

Amelia did as she was told, wishing with all her heart that Grayson was already there. She needed him, needed someone to hold her hand through this.

"It's going to be all right," Levi said from her other side. "She's strong."

She quickly glanced up at him, not realizing that he'd

gotten out of the truck. His words brought her some relief. When Levi said things like that, they weren't just words meant to make her feel better. He really could sense those things with his spirit magic.

It was by pure chance that he'd been up at Silas's that evening. Silas had already taken off to work on his next project. Levi had only been at his house to pick up some supplies he needed for Cappy, who was staying with Levi while Silas was out of town. He'd happened to be headed back to town when he'd spotted her clutching her back and fumbling to get into her car. Once he realized what the problem was, he'd insisted on driving her. Amelia was relieved and grateful.

Levi took her hand in his and walked into the clinic with her and Martin Whipple.

"Thank you," she said to the teenager. "I don't know how I would've made it without you."

"There's no need to worry about that," he said. "I'm just glad I was there to help."

"Hold that door open for me, Levi," Martin said when they got to one of the exam rooms.

Levi did as he was told and then hovered in the doorway as Martin wheeled Amelia to the exam table. "Do you want me to stay?" His face was a bit pale as he ran a hand over his head nervously.

Amelia wanted to say yes because she didn't want to be alone, but the reality was she needed to get undressed, and there was no way Levi could stay for the exam. She shook her head. "It's okay, Levi. Thank you again."

"I'll be just outside," he said and then disappeared.

Gerry appeared and strode into the room the moment Levi left. She had short gray hair and was wearing an apron over her long skirt and peasant blouse instead of a white physician's coat. "I've got it from here, Martin."

Her husband nodded and quickly left the room, closing the door behind him.

"All right, now, tell me what's wrong," Gerry said, opening the file she had in her hands.

"There's some light bleeding, and my lower back aches so much it's hard to stand up straight," Amelia said.

"How light and for how long have you had the bleeding?"

"It started today after I got home from work. My backache started earlier today, and then I slipped on the porch stairs when I was going to get my mail. That's when everything went to hell. I could hardly even move, but I hobbled inside. Then there was bleeding and I..." She trailed off. "Is my baby going to be okay?"

"I'm going to do everything I can," Gerry said. "Tell me about your back hurting earlier. Did anything happen?"

"I don't know if you remember, but a couple days ago, I tried to pick up a log and hurt my back. Levi actually helped with the spasm and everything was fine... until today. I'm not sure if it's related. My back hurts, but I'm worried about the bleeding. I'm terrified I hurt the baby." Her voice cracked on the word baby.

"Okay, let's not panic yet. First, we need to get you undressed so I can do the exam. Then we'll go from there." Gerry patted Amelia's knee and then squeezed her hand as tears spilled down Amelia's cheeks.

"Up on your feet. Let's get this gown on you." Gerry carefully and tenderly helped Amelia into the gown before guiding her back onto the table. "Just relax. I've got you from here, okay?"

"Okay," Amelia said, holding her abdomen and sniffling

through her tears. What had she been thinking? She knew the deck was slick. Why wasn't she being more careful during this pregnancy? She'd heard that some bleeding could be normal. But not when someone slipped on slick steps. Right? Her mind was filled with all the worst possible scenarios, and she kept glancing at the door, wondering why Grayson wasn't there yet. All she wanted was to see his face and for the healer to tell her everything would be fine.

"I'm going to run my fingers over your back to get an assessment of what's going on there. If anything hurts, let me know," the healer said.

Amelia nodded. "Right now it's just a dull ache."

"Okay. That's good." She opened the back of the gown and tenderly probed at Amelia's spine. When Gerry got to her lower back and pressed gingerly on the right side, Amelia sucked in a sharp breath. "That hurts, right?" Gerry said.

"Yes. When you pressed on it, I got a sharp pain down my leg."

"Okay. That's good to know." She repeated the procedure on the other side, but this time it felt no different than the persistent dull ache. "It looks like the pain in your back is due to irritating your sciatic nerve. There are a number of things you can do to alleviate the pain, such as stretches, massage, and alternating heat and ice packs. Normally, I could give you a potion that would help, but there's nothing strong enough that will touch the sciatica that's safe for pregnancies. The other remedies won't do much other than make you sleepy." She gave Amelia a sympathetic smile. "Looks like you're going to have to let it heal without a witch's brew."

"That's it?" Amelia asked, a little irritated. "Stretches, massage, and ice packs?" She could've gotten that advice off the internet. Her irritation turned to fear when she added, "What about the bleeding? What if I hurt my baby?"

"That's not likely," Gerry said soothingly. "But we're going to do an exam, and then I'll do an ultrasound to check on your little one. Go ahead and lie back and just relax."

Relax. Why did healers always say that right when they were getting ready to stick their instruments up your hoo-ha? As if anyone could relax under those circumstances. Besides, she wouldn't be calm until she knew her little one was healthy.

The healer did her thing, poking Amelia with a cold instrument and making indiscernible noises. By the time she was done, Amelia was so nervous she was shaking.

"Oh, honey. Are you cold? I can get Martin to adjust the heat."

Amelia shook her head. "No. Just anxious."

Gerry nodded. "I see. Well, you really can relax. Everything looks okay. The bleeding isn't that much, and I'm going to guess it was a result of overextending yourself a bit when you irritated that nerve. We're going to do that ultrasound now, but I really don't think there is anything to worry about."

"Okay." Amelia closed her eyes and let out a long breath. Nothing to worry about. She kept repeating the mantra in her mind as Gerry got the ultrasound machine going. It wasn't long before she heard the strong pulse of a heartbeat on the monitor. It was only then that Amelia felt all the tension drain from her body and let the tears fall unchecked. The fear and adrenaline had done a number on her, and now she was crashing.

There was a knock on the door, followed by Martin poking his head in. "There's a Grayson Riley here. Says he's the daddy. Do you want me to let him in?"

"Yes," Amelia said immediately.

The door opened wider and Grayson rushed in, his face white and etched with fear. "Are they okay?" he asked Gerry. "Amelia and the baby?" His gaze locked on Amelia's, and before Gerry gave an answer, he rushed to her side, grabbing one of her hands with both of his. "Are you all right?"

"I think so," Amelia said, the tears streaming faster now that Grayson was there.

His brow furrowed and panic flashed in his eyes, no doubt from her uncontrollable crying.

"Amelia and the baby are perfectly fine, Mr. Riley," Gerry said kindly. "It appears Amelia tweaked her back and overextended herself a little. Lifting too much weight or irritating the area can sometimes cause bleeding. I'm going to send her home with strict instructions that she stay off her feet for at least the next week. If the bleeding gets any worse or doesn't stop by tomorrow, call me. I'll give you my private number." She shifted her focus to Amelia. "So stay off your feet, don't do anything strenuous, watch the bleeding, and absolutely no sex until we're sure you're in the clear. Understand?"

Amelia nodded and felt her cheeks flush red. She didn't know why she was so embarrassed that the healer had brought up sex. Grayson was the father after all. It made sense for her to assume they were still together in that way.

"Understood," Grayson said. "Don't worry. I'll take care of her."

"I'm sure you will," Healer Gerry said. "Hot cocoa and cake wouldn't hurt either," she said with a wink.

Amelia, who was sitting up and holding the front of her gown to her chest, laughed. "Is that a prescription for the remainder of my pregnancy?"

"Yes. Need that in writing?" she asked.

Amelia nodded and grinned at Grayson as he rolled his eyes. But he smiled at her, showing that he was a good sport.

"You can get dressed now," Gerry said. "Do you need help or is daddy here going to do that?"

"I'll help," Grayson said before Amelia could answer.

"Good. I actually am going to prescribe some prenatal herbs specifically to help with the bleeding, and I'll give you a tip sheet on what kind of stretches to do. Take your time getting dressed, and when you're ready, I'll have this stuff for you at the front desk."

"Thank you, Healer Whipple," Grayson said, shaking her hand. "We appreciate your help so much."

Amelia nodded, still unable to control the few tears spilling down her cheeks. She wiped at them and said, "He's right. Thank you for getting me in so soon."

"Any time. This is what I'm here for." She slipped out of the exam room and closed the door softly behind her.

"Oh, my gods." Amelia covered her face with her hands. "I am such an idiot."

"No you aren't." Grayson sat on the exam table next to her, wrapping his arm around her shoulders. "You slipped and tweaked your back. It happens to everyone."

"But I was just going about my life as if I'm not pregnant. I was even still working at the station. What if there'd been a fire? Was I just going to go try to put it out and ignore the fact that I have this child inside of me?"

"I doubt that. Pretty sure your bosses would've ordered you to stay back from the flames while you worked on communications or whatever logistics you badasses need when fighting fires."

She let out a laugh that turned into a hiccup and then

concentrated on breathing until she had herself under control. "I don't think I qualify as a badass at the moment."

"I'll be the judge of that. Now stand up and let me get you dressed so that I can take you home."

She did as he asked and felt her heart flutter at his tender touch. He was so careful with her it nearly made her cry again.

"You still doing all right?" he asked as he buttoned her jeans for her.

"Yeah. Just shaken up."

"I bet." He kissed her temple, finished dressing her, and then even tied her shoes. "Okay, Mama. You look ready."

She shrugged into her jacket, but before she moved to the door, she flung her arms around him. "I'm so glad you came."

"Why wouldn't I have come?" he asked, bewildered.

She glanced up at him, her lips turned into a frown. "Well, I heard you were on a date. I—"

"Amelia," he said earnestly. "I absolutely was not on a date. As for Kira, like I told your voicemail, she showed up here unannounced. I had no idea she'd come here. But she is my oldest friend and was in a certain amount of distress, so I couldn't kick her out, no matter how much my gut was telling me to."

"You mean Katy," Amelia said.

"No, I mean Kira. Katy is her stage name." He slipped his fingers through hers and kissed the back of her hand. "It's a long story, and the reason I didn't tell you before is because I have an NDA in place. But since she told you herself, that no longer applies. If you'll let me, I'd like to take you home, make you something to eat if you're hungry, and then explain my friendship with Kira. But only if you're up for it. I don't want you to have to deal with any of it if you just need peace and quiet."

"No. I want to know." She slipped her arm around his waist and leaned into his chest. It was in that moment that all of her anxiety eased, and she was ready to accept whatever it was Grayson had to offer. Because it was clear that, no matter what she told herself, she needed this man in her life. His presence just made her feel safe and cared for in a way that she'd never really experienced before. "I'm supposed to be on bedrest for the next week, so when we get home, you can wait on me while I pretend your entire existence is for the purpose of pleasing me."

Heat flashed in his dark eyes, and a spark of electricity zoomed through her body, making her want to plaster herself to him. Instead, she cleared her throat and said, "That might have come out more sexual than I intended. Normally I'd just roll with it, but you heard Healer Gerry. Absolutely no sex."

Grayson groaned and mumbled something about it being a long five months, but then he kissed her temple again before ordering her into the wheelchair Martin had left behind.

"I can walk," she said stubbornly.

"It's either that, or I'm carrying you out of here. You heard the woman. Off your feet for the next week."

When she hesitated to get into the chair, Grayson took matters into his own hands and swept her up into his arms.

She protested, but when it was clear he wouldn't be deterred as he strode down the hallway, she gave in and rested her head against his strong shoulder. Then she mentally congratulated herself for refusing the wheelchair, because there simply wasn't anything better than being manhandled by Grayson Riley.

CHAPTER 16

After grabbing Amelia's herbs and information packet, Grayson thanked Levi and promised to be available for anything the young man needed in the future. Then Grayson carried Amelia out to his SUV, placed her in the passenger seat, and secured her seatbelt as if she were a helpless child and then drove her straight home, desperate to keep her safe and off her feet.

Once they were parked in her driveway, Grayson opened the SUV passenger door, held his arms wide open and said, "Hop in."

Amelia eyed him and shook her head as a small smile claimed her lips. "You're enjoying this entirely too much."

"So are you," he countered.

Amusement danced in her eyes, and it warmed him to the core. Earlier, when he'd walked into that exam room and seen her so upset, his heart had nearly stopped. He'd been sure that they were going to tell him that she'd lost the baby. But then Healer Whipple had made it clear everything was fine and all Amelia had to do was rest. He hadn't even realized just how scared he was until he'd heard those reassuring words. His entire body had been curled tight, as if protecting him from a terrible fate. But then the tension drained away, and all he wanted to do was hold Amelia and reassure her that nothing was going to happen to their baby.

Grayson waited as Amelia unlocked her door and then smiled to himself when he carried her over the threshold. Would that be them on their wedding day sometime in the future? He had no idea if they were destined for such a union, but he liked to think it was possible.

"What are you smiling about?" she asked.

"The future." He kicked the door closed and headed straight for her room. After placing her gently on her bed, he removed her shoes and then climbed onto the bed with her.

"Is this the way it's going to be?" she asked, suddenly looking serious.

He laid down beside her and tucked one of her dark curls behind her ear. "What do you mean?"

"This." She waved at him. "You. When we're together, you're attentive and supportive and you make me feel... cherished. But then you leave, and you have this whole other history and life that revolves around a literal movie star, and that just seems really big. I'm having a hard time wrapping my head around the fact that Katy Carmichael is at your house right now, probably waiting in your bed so that you two can cuddle." She practically spit out the word *cuddle*.

Grayson sat up, needing to collect his thoughts. She'd just said a mouthful, and he needed to process her words before he responded.

After a moment, Amelia pushed herself up and leaned against the pillows piled up against her headboard. "I didn't mean to accuse you of anything," she explained. "Katy said that you two often sleep in the same bed because you like to cuddle."

He let out a bark of humorless laughter. "Did she? That's interesting." He decided it was a damned good thing that Kira wasn't there in Amelia's house, because he seriously didn't know if he'd be able to keep his cool. What the hell was she thinking, saying something like that to Amelia?

"Is it not true?" Her eyes were wide with both suspicion and trepidation.

"No. At least not recently." He ran a hand through his hair, frustrated by that damned NDA. He wasn't supposed to be talking about his relationship with Kira, aka Katy Carmichael. But he'd already confided enough to Amelia that, surely, she had already put two and two together and knew that he'd dated her once upon a time. This was Kira's fault. If she hadn't shown up and ambushed Amelia, he wouldn't feel he had to explain. At least not yet.

"Not recently?" Amelia squeaked. "So not since you left New York?"

"What? No!" He took a deep breath to give himself a second to settle his thoughts. "No," he said again, this time feeling calmer. "If you've listened to your voicemail, you know that Kira is Katy's given name and that she's the friend I've been telling you about. Which means you already know that I dated her when we were younger. It wasn't for that long, but we remained friends. Close friends. In those early years, we really only had each other to lean on. So yes, even after we were no longer an item, sometimes we cuddled when we needed comfort from someone. But it hasn't been like that in a very long time."

"So this was like, maybe ten years ago?" she asked, looking relieved.

Grayson nodded. It was close enough.

Amelia frowned. "So why did she taunt me with that yesterday?"

"Jealousy?" he guessed. "After college, I went to work for a PR company. I was there for a little over a year before she convinced me to come work for her full-time. That's when she had me sign an NDA that included not talking about our relationship. Part of her image as a young star on the rise was always to appear available. Even the hint of a relationship was a problem for her. Which, at the time, was fine with me. I wasn't interested in being in the tabloids and didn't want the general public always wondering if we were together. We weren't. But she had me all to herself for a lot of years. I suspect she thinks I left her and New York for you."

"Are you saying you didn't?"

"No. Not saying that at all." He held his hand out to her and was gratified when she took it. He squeezed her fingers and stroked the back of her hand with his thumb. "I did regret ending things with you. But there are other, unrelated reasons why I left New York when I did and told Kira I wasn't going to work for her anymore. I meant it when I told her I was done… for good this time."

"Yet, she's at your house right now," Amelia said, staring at the wall behind him. But she didn't let go of his hand.

"Yes," he said with a sigh. "She's still that girl I lived next to all those years ago even if I have a hard time seeing her underneath her celebrity persona sometimes. I don't work for her anymore. I won't go back to that. I can't. But I still care about what happens to her."

Amelia's head popped up, and she stared him in the eye when she asked, "Are you in love with her?"

"No," he said with zero hesitation.

"Is she in love with you?"

He laughed. "No. Kira doesn't know how to love anyone but herself. She cares about me. Of that, I'm sure. But love? I'm not sure she knows how to love someone else." He felt like a traitor saying that. But it was what he'd concluded when they broke up all those years ago and again when he'd walked away from her on New Year's Day. When she was away from acting and the press, he often saw glimpses of the girl he'd known. Unfortunately for him, that didn't happen often. Her entire world revolved around landing the next big role. It wasn't something he'd willingly sign up for again.

"Those words seem pretty harsh coming from the person who's supposed to be her best friend."

Grayson stared into Amelia's large brown eyes and saw nothing but compassion staring back at him. He'd expected judgment but should've known better. Amelia wasn't one for rushing to judgment. It was likely the only reason he still had a chance with her. "They are. I wish I could just tell you everything that has gone down with her and her friends, but on the other hand, I'm almost relieved that I can't. It's probably both worse and not quite as bad as you think. Anyway, can we say that I used to make unflattering stories go away and find ways to boost her public image and leave it at that?"

"That sounds like a dreadful existence, Grayson," she said, moving over and laying her head on his shoulder.

"It was. But she's been my only family for a long time. I wanted to help her and make her life easier. I felt needed, which was sort of a drug for a guy who doesn't have many people in his life." He shrugged, leaning into the vulnerable state he'd finally allowed himself to experience. "Like most drugs, the situation became toxic, and I probably should've walked away sooner, but I didn't know how. It wasn't until after I met you that I learned how I should be treated. You showed me that without even trying. It's just who you are."

"Oh, Grayson," she whispered, wrapping her arms around him and holding on tightly. "You deserve so much love. I'm so sorry your parents were taken from you so soon and that those around you haven't had the tools to care for you the way you deserve to be cared for."

"I'm okay," he said thickly. He was surprised that it didn't bother him for her to see him so clearly. But he also didn't want her to think he was broken. A little scarred maybe, but not broken.

"I know you are. That's what's so remarkable. Thank you for being honest. I know there are things you can't tell me, and that's okay. You have a past that doesn't involve me. Let's just move forward from here. Okay?"

He let out a sigh of relief and gathered her close. "I can't think of anything I want more."

"Just promise me one thing?"

"What's that?" he asked, willing to give her anything in that moment.

"Be honest with me about whatever's going on with you and Kira. Like I said, I know there are things you can't tell me, and I'm fine with that. I honestly don't need the drama." She pressed a hand to her belly and smiled softly. "I just care about what's happening from this point forward. If she's going to be in your life, which it appears she is, then just don't let me be ambushed by anything, okay?"

"I'll try," he said, meaning it. "I can't promise that won't happen because her life is a circus, and you've already seen a bit of how she behaves when she's spiraling, but…" He trailed off, realizing he was about to make excuses for his old friend. She'd deliberately manipulated Amelia into thinking things that weren't true, all to appease her own ego. He wasn't going to stand for that again. Amelia was who he cared about, who he wanted to be with, and who he wanted to share a life with. Letting Kira railroad any of that wasn't acceptable. "You know what? Forget that. If she can't treat you with respect, then she won't be in our lives."

She raised both of her eyebrows. "You'd cut off contact with her for me?"

"Yes," he said without hesitation.

"I don't want you to do that," she said softly. "It can't be because of me. I don't want to be the person who comes between you and someone you care about."

And that was just one of the reasons he loved her so much. Her empathy, combined with her strength, drew him in and fascinated him. "I appreciate that," he said and kissed the top of her head. "But it wouldn't only be for you. It'd be for me, too. I want a life like my parents had before the accident. It was full of love and family and living an authentic life. That's not Kira's existence. And I'm starting to realize it likely never will be. I've been holding onto her because of our past. But if holding onto her ruins my future, than I have to learn to let go. Like you said, it's okay to realize that people are in your life for a while for a reason, but every relationship isn't meant to last forever."

She stared up at him and placed her palm over his heart. "Just know that I'll never ask you to choose. Whatever you decide is right for you, I'll support your decision."

Tears stung Grayson's eyes. He'd never had someone like her in his corner before. She only wanted what was best for him. That rang true in everything she said and did, and it had from the beginning. "Amelia?"

"Yeah?"

He swallowed hard, clearing the lump in his throat.

Emotion threatened to overwhelm him, but when he spoke the words, they were clear and full of truth. "I love you."

Tears shone in her eyes as she stared up at him. "Do you mean it?"

He nodded. "I've known ever since I walked away from you. I thought we needed more time, that things might be rushed, and maybe they are. But it's how I feel, and you deserve to know."

She let out a tiny sob of emotion and whispered, "I love you, too, Grayson Riley. I love you, too."

CHAPTER 17

Amelia woke snuggled in Grayson's arms. The dim morning light shown through the window, indicating it was just after sunrise. She'd never been much of an early riser, but ever since she'd become pregnant, her internal clock had reset, and now she was up with the birds more often than not.

She blinked the sleep from her eyes and studied Grayson as he slept. He seemed so peaceful and content in a way he hadn't been when they were together before. The worry lines in his forehead had been smoothed away, and the tension in his limbs had eased. It warmed her all the way to her toes to think them coming together had something to do with that.

Doing her best not to rouse him, she slipped from the bed to make her way to the bathroom. Relief rushed through her when she realized the herbs had worked and the bleeding had stopped. She was filled with gratitude for Healer Whipple and made a mental note to text an update and a thank you once it was office hours.

After brushing her teeth and finishing her business in the

bathroom, Amelia slipped back into bed, snuggling in close to Grayson. He let out a contented sigh, and much to her surprise, it wasn't long before she fell back into slumber.

A rustling of the bedcovers woke Amelia from her morning nap, and a warm hand rested on her hip. His breath smelled of mint toothpaste as Grayson's low voice whispered, "Morning, gorgeous."

"Morning." She rolled over and smiled up at his handsome face. "How did you sleep?"

"Better than I have in months. You? Are you feeling okay?" His hand moved to rest on her belly.

"Feeling perfect. The herbs worked. There was no bleeding this morning and while my back is stiff, I can at least move around without shooting pain down my leg."

He let out a sigh of relief and nuzzled her neck before pressing a soft kiss just below her ear. "That's the best news I've ever heard."

Amelia ran her fingers through his soft hair, just enjoying lying with him. She'd really missed this, the physical connection they shared even when they weren't doing anything more than just touching each other.

"Damn, that feels good."

"Mm-hmm," she agreed.

He raised his head and stared down at her lips.

She gave him a soft smile and said, "Kiss me, Grayson."

He didn't hesitate. His lips brushed against hers, and she immediately opened to him. He tasted of mint and man and everything she'd ever wanted in life. Grayson pressed his palm to her cheek and deepened the kiss, taking her mouth like a starving man. They kissed for a long time, touching and exploring each other's skin, but neither took it further. Eventually Grayson pulled back, slightly out of breath, and said, "I think maybe we should stop here before we take it too far."

Amelia trailed her fingers down his chest and didn't stop until she got to the waistband of his boxers. "Just because we can't have sex doesn't mean we can't do other things. It doesn't mean I can't please you."

Grayson let out a groan and shifted to his back as he covered his eyes with one hand. "You have no idea how much I want to say yes to that." He lowered his arm and stared up at her as he tucked one of her curls behind her ear. "But I'd really like to wait until we're both able to participate."

She shook her head. "Pleasing you *is* me participating." Then her hand slipped into his boxers, and they got lost in their kisses again. It didn't take long until he let out another groan, this one of pure pleasure.

Pleased with herself, Amelia gave him one last kiss and then slipped out of bed and headed to the shower. It didn't surprise her when the door opened and Grayson slipped in with her. Showering together had always been a favorite activity of his.

"I was wondering if you'd join me," she said, glancing at him over her shoulder.

Grayson slipped his arms around her, kissed her shoulder, and said, "I might not be able to please you the way I want to, but I sure as hell can take care of you in other ways."

"Oh? How's that?"

"Like this." Grayson grabbed a bottle out of her shower caddy and went to work on shampooing her hair. He took his time massaging her scalp, washing every inch of her skin, and generally worshiping her body without defying the healer's orders. By the time they stepped out of the shower, Amelia was warm and happy and had never felt more cherished.

"Okay, go relax on the couch," Grayson said. "I'm going to make breakfast."

"I can help," she said.

He raised one eyebrow. "Absolutely not. You heard Healer Whipple. You're to stay off your feet for the next week." He pointed toward the living room. "Go, or you're getting oatmeal for breakfast instead of waffles."

She held up her hands in defeat. "Okay. You're right. I guess I'm a terrible patient." And she really was. Just the day before she was berating herself for not being more careful with her pregnancy. She just felt so good that morning that she'd momentarily forgotten that she was to take it as easy as possible. "I promise not to get up for anything. But do you think you could make coffee a priority? I'm getting a little desperate."

"Of course." He chuckled, kissed the top of her head, and guided her to the living room, making sure she was comfortable on the couch before he disappeared into the kitchen, while she called the fire station to let them know she was on bed rest for the week.

After Grayson rescheduled his appointments, they spent the rest of the day at her house, with Grayson hovering over Amelia, making sure she was comfortable, fed, and entertained with card games and movies. It was the perfect way to spend a chilly winter day.

By the time the evening rolled around, they were both cuddled up on the couch with Grayson's arm around Amelia and her head tucked against his shoulder.

"Grayson?" Amelia asked.

"Yeah."

"If you were in PR since you graduated college, how did

you end up becoming an account rep for a beverage distributer?"

"It's kind of a funny story, actually." He let out a soft chuckle. "A few years ago, I parted ways with Kira and went to work for a PR firm in Boston. I was living downtown and used to frequent this neighborhood bar a few times a week just to get out a bit. Every Thursday night, this guy used to come in and sit next to me. We talked about everything from sports to movies to politics. Then one day he comes in and asks if he can buy me a drink. I honestly thought he was hitting on me."

"He wasn't?" she asked.

"Nope." Grayson laughed. "I stammered all over my words because I was so caught off guard that I made a complete fool of myself. I said something about how that was really nice of him, but I wasn't looking to date or hook up with anyone."

"What did he say?"

"He just threw his head back and laughed. Then he ordered the beer, had me try it, and asked what I thought." Grayson shrugged one shoulder. "I told him it was the best thing to pass my lips since I made out with Tyler Foster in the ninth grade. Of course, he thought Tyler was a guy and it was just a big cluster of mistaken communication and sexual identity. Eventually, he said he didn't give a damn who I slept with as long as it wasn't him because he already had a wife."

Amelia turned to watch him, enjoying the humor in his expression. He never looked like that when he talked about his past. It was a refreshing change.

"Anyway, over the next few months, he was constantly asking me to try different beers and wines. Not everything was a winner, but there were quite a few. I kinda just thought he liked taste-testing stuff, and I was happy to go along. But eventually he told me he owned a distribution company, and that my taste was impeccable. That everything I liked always ended up being a winner for them. He handed me his card and said if I ever wanted to switch jobs, I had a place with them. I pocketed it and thanked him but told him I liked my job. Shortly after that I went back to work for Kira. Two years later I called him, and he offered me any territory I wanted. That's how I ended up here."

"That's... something," she said.

He shrugged. "After I took this job, he told me he knew we'd end up working together one day, he just didn't know when."

"Another spirit witch?"

Grayson nodded. "I think that might have been one of those mystical connections."

Amelia squeezed his hand. "I think you're right. Thank him for me one day, okay? The best thing that's happened to me was when you walked back into my life."

Grayson opened his mouth to answer her, but there was a loud knock on the door that cut him off. "Are you expecting anyone?"

She shook her head.

He got up, and before he even answered the door, he let out a curse.

"What is it?"

"Not what, who." He gave her a pained look. "Kira's here."

"Why?" Amelia asked, all the warm feelings of the day vanishing. But then she suddenly remembered that she'd had plans with Kira at the Cozy Cave that night and let out a curse of her own.

"I know. I'm sorry. I'll make her go away," Grayson said, already reaching for the doorknob.

"No, don't." Amelia said quickly. "I owe her an apology."

"What? Why?" he asked just as the knocking started again.

"We had plans tonight. I stood her up and forgot to send her a message. Open the door, Grayson. It's cold out there."

He let out a groan, clearly unhappy at the turn of events, but he did as she asked.

Katy Carmichael stood on Amelia's front porch, dressed in tight jeans, an oversized sweater, and a faux fur white jacket that looked about two sizes too big for her petite frame. "Grayson, I figured you must be here," she said with a bright smile. "But when you didn't answer any of my texts, I couldn't be sure."

"Is that why you're here?" he asked coolly. "Because I didn't answer you?"

"Of course not. Don't flatter yourself." She brushed past him and walked into the house without being invited. "I'm here because Amelia and I had a date. When she didn't show up for our dinner, I heard through the grapevine that she's on bedrest, so I decided the best thing to do was to bring dinner to her." She beamed at Amelia. "I'm glad to see he's taking care of you. I hope you don't mind the intrusion, but I did bring dinner for three, hoping we can still get to know each other."

Amelia stared at the star, both speechless at her audacity to just barge in and also slightly guilty for standing her up. "Hi, Katy. I'm really sorry. I should've gotten your number from Grayson and let you know I couldn't make it. Please, come in and have a seat." She glanced at Grayson. "Get Katy something to drink, will you?"

Grayson pressed his lips into a thin line, clearly not happy with this turn of events. Still, he turned his attention to Katy and said, "Amelia doesn't have any alcohol in the house. Is sparkling water okay? Or I can make you coffee or tea."

"Sparkling water is perfect," she said with a bright smile. He nodded, and as Katy watched him walk toward the kitchen, she added, "Hey, Grayson?"

He paused and glanced back at her. "What?"

"Try to remember that you love me while you're in there. Okay?"

Grayson rolled his eyes and disappeared into the other room.

"He's just cranky because I showed up unannounced," Katy said, placing the takeout on the coffee table and sitting next to Amelia. "He'll get over it soon enough."

Amelia was well aware that wasn't the only reason he was annoyed, but she wasn't going to get into it with the actress. As long as Katy left Amelia out of it, Amelia had no desire to come between the two of them. She cleared her throat. "So, how are you enjoying Keating Hollow? Have you had a chance to see much of it?"

She laughed. "Oh, yes. The brewery, the café, the winery, the spa, and even the music store. The owner there, Chad, is that his name?"

Amelia nodded. "Yes, he's Hope's husband. She works at the spa."

"*Fascinating*," she said in an exaggerated tone that made Amelia wonder if she was mocking her. "He is a delicious piece of man-candy, isn't he? The way he was demonstrating the guitar I inquired about…" She fanned herself with her hand. "Too bad he's already taken. I think we could've had a hot weekend together."

"Sure," Amelia said just to be polite. She liked gossiping about boys just as much as the next girl, but there was something off about the interaction with Katy that Amelia just couldn't put her finger on. "You play guitar?"

She shook her head. "No, but there's a role in a movie that I want and the lead plays. If I could get the basics down, that will probably help convince the casting director that I'm the right fit." Her entire demeanor had changed when talking about her career. She was much more natural and relaxed. Just more comfortable in her skin.

Amelia decided to keep the conversation focused on her work. It seemed to be a better path than Keating Hollow. "That's pretty cool. How much time do you have to learn?"

She shrugged. "A few weeks I think."

"That should be enough to at least make it look like you know what you're doing. Wait here a minute. I'll be right back." Amelia swung her legs off the couch and started to get to her feet.

A firm hand landed on her shoulder. It wasn't heavy enough to keep her in place, just enough to make her pause and look up at Grayson.

"What?" she asked.

"Unless you're headed to the bathroom, whatever it is you need, I'll get it," Grayson said as he handed Katy her drink.

Amelia let out a long-suffering sigh. This bedrest thing was for the birds. Thankfully he hadn't taken Healer Whipple literally and forced her to actually stay in bed all day. Instead, she was relegated to the couch. "My guitar is in the nursery in the closet. Can you get it for me?"

"Sure," he said without hesitation and left the room again.

"You play?" Katy asked, her eyes lighting with interest.

"Some. I learned as a teenager." Amelia smiled shyly. It was a hobby she didn't talk about often, since playing the guitar was something she just did for herself. She'd never had dreams of being a professional musician or anything like that. It was more of a way to unwind at the end of the day and to keep her hands busy.

Grayson returned with the instrument and handed it to Amelia. She smiled gratefully up at him. "Thank you."

"Of course." He went to work on removing the takeout from the bags, while Amelia took a moment to strum a few chords before breaking into "Royals" by Lorde.

"Wow, that's pretty good," Katy said, sounding impressed.

"Thanks. After dinner, I'd be happy to show you a few things if you'd like. You'll still need lessons, but at least you could get hand positioning down."

"That would be wonderful," she said, looking pleased. Then she glanced at the coffee table and frowned. "Looks like we need plates and some silverware." She got to her feet and said, "I'll find them."

Amelia and Grayson watched her go and then turned to each other. Amelia said, "She's quite the contradiction, isn't she?"

"You can say that again." He reached out and squeezed her hand. "Thank you for being you."

She squeezed back. "Ditto."

Dinner was filled with celebrity gossip and talk of different movies and shows Katy had done. The actress was in her element, and if Amelia was honest, very charming when telling her stories. By the time they were done eating, Amelia could see why she was so popular with her fans and hoped they'd eventually find a way to be friends.

"I'll clean up," Grayson said, grabbing the plates and takeout trays.

They both watched him walk away. Amelia smiled to herself. A month ago, she'd never have imagined that they'd find their way back together, but here they were with Grayson taking such good care of her. It was like a dream. A wonderful, love-filled dream.

"You know he'll never last here, right?" Katy said.

"What?" Amelia turned to study Grayson's friend. "What do you mean?"

"This town. Keating Hollow. It's too small town." She shrugged as if what she was saying was obvious. "He's spent his entire adult life in the city, surrounded by powerful people in the business. This life he's tried to start here, being a beverage account rep? It's not him. Not at all. He thrives on the cutthroat business of celebrity public relations. I doubt you've ever seen him after he's killed a big story or planted one to help my star grow. It's almost like a drug, knowing you've outsmarted the media like that. He tried to walk away once before. That only lasted a few weeks. I honestly wouldn't be surprised if he's back in the city within the month."

Amelia gaped at her. Had she seriously just sat there and matter-of-factly told Amelia that the life she was looking to build with Grayson was a fantasy?

Katy's phone buzzed. She glanced down at it and frowned. After sending a text back, she gave Amelia an apologetic smile. "Listen, thanks for the offer to show me the guitar, but it looks like I'm going to have to take off. My business manager is on a tear about something." She hurried to the door, and on her way out, she said, "Tell Grayson I'll talk to him soon."

The door slammed closed and Amelia stared at it. There was no doubt the actress wasn't going to give up Grayson easily. She just wondered what Katy would do next to try to lure him back to her.

Amelia's vision blurred, and she clutched the arm of the couch, wondering if she was getting ready to pass out. But then the vision hit.

Grayson stood in an unfamiliar bedroom. The king-size bed had a white satin comforter accented with furry pink pillows. The ornate white headboard looked like something out of *Lifestyles of the Rich and Famous*. Grayson moved toward the window with his arms outstretched, and a moment later, Katy Carmichael stepped into his embrace. They stood there holding onto each other, her head pressed to his chest while he caressed her hair and kissed the top of her head.

"I'm here now, Kira. You don't have to worry about a thing. I'll take care of you," he said.

She tilted her head up so she could look at him, and then she kissed him.

Amelia's vision blurred once more, and just like that she was sitting in her living room still staring at the door, her heart racing so fast she thought it would beat right out of her chest.

"What is it?" Grayson asked, sitting on the sofa to face her. "What happened?"

Amelia swallowed hard, trying to keep the tears from pooling in her eyes. "It's not over between you two," she forced out.

"Between who? Me and Kira?"

She nodded. "I had a vision. You're going back to her. Holly had one, too. I just…" She shook her head. "I don't know how to do this, knowing that I'll always have to share this part of you."

Grayson grabbed both of her hands and stared at her earnestly. "Listen to me, Amelia Holiday. I'm in love with you. Not Kira. Understand?"

She nodded, because she really did believe him.

"Neither of us can predict the future. Those visions… I can't control what you or anyone else sees. But I can control what I do. And I'm making a promise right here and now that you and our child come first. Do you understand what I'm saying?"

She nodded again, this time, unable to stop the tears from rolling down her cheeks.

"I choose you. I'll always choose you." He pulled her into his arms and held her, just as he'd held Katy in her vision. "I choose you," he whispered again, his voice thick with emotions.

Amelia clung to him, desperate to believe him. But in her heart, she knew their time was limited.

CHAPTER 18

For the second day in a row, Grayson woke with Amelia in his arms. After Kira left the night before, they'd had an emotional but quiet evening. They'd lain on the couch together with Amelia leaning against his chest while they watched some movie that he didn't even recall. He'd just been happy to have her near and trusting him to take care of her.

He'd have been happy to keep her wrapped in his arms for forever, but it was a new day and Grayson had a job to do. After carefully slipping out of her bed so as not to wake her, he quickly cleaned up and then went about making her breakfast. Once he had an omelet made and coffee in hand, he slipped back into her bedroom and sat next to her on the bed. The movement roused her, and she blinked sleepily at him.

"Morning," she said, her hair mussed and her cheeks rosy from sleep.

Gods, she was adorable. "Morning." He leaned down and gave her a gentle kiss. "I have to get home and get changed for work. But if it's okay with you, when I get back into town this afternoon, I'd like to pack a bag and stay here for the rest of the week."

She pressed her hand to his cheek. "It's more than okay." She lifted her head and scented the air. "Is that coffee I smell?"

"Yes. I made you breakfast." He gestured to the omelet and the coffee on her nightstand. "I also brought you the remote and that book you had in the living room, so you can stay right here for as long as you want."

"You've just thought of everything, haven't you?" Her eyes twinkled with amusement.

"I hope so." He pressed a kiss to her forehead. "Call me if you need anything. Or even if you're just bored. I only have two appointments, but I will be driving a lot today so it's likely you won't be interrupting me." He'd managed to rearrange his schedule so that he only needed to be out in the field for half the day.

"I'm sure I'll be fine. Those herbs Healer Whipple prescribed really did help with the bleeding."

"How about your back?" he asked, narrowing his eyes in suspicion. She'd been moving slowly and using her hand to support her back when she moved between the couch and the bedroom the night before.

"It's still stiff, but I'll work on those stretching exercises. Don't worry about me. What's going to happen while I'm laid up in bed?"

He let out a humorless chuckle. "Let's not temp fate by asking that question, all right?"

Her smile was soft as she gazed up at him. "Fair enough. But really, I'm doing so much better. Now go so you can get back here and continue your hovering."

Grayson glanced at her breakfast. "Looks like you're not suffering too much from my attention."

Amelia grinned, cupped both of his cheeks with her palms and pulled him down for a kiss. When they finally pulled apart, she said, "No. Not suffering at all."

∽

GRAYSON FELT strange walking into his house. It had only taken a few days for Amelia's place to feel more like home than his rental did. His house was cold and impersonal, while hers just felt right in a way that he was certain had everything to do with her presence and nothing at all to do with the décor.

He strode straight to his bathroom, took a quick shower, and then filled a duffel with the clothes he'd need for the rest of the week. He was on his way back out when he heard footsteps behind him.

"You're not leaving already, are you?" Kira asked.

He turned to look at her and frowned. Her hair was in a ponytail, and she wore a pair of old sweatpants with a Hello Kitty T-shirt he thought he remembered from when they had just moved to New York. But what really surprised him were the dark circles under her eyes. "Have you slept at all?"

"Not really." She curled up in the corner of the couch and asked, "Do you have a few minutes to talk before you go back to her?"

"I was on my way out to work."

She glanced at the duffel in his hand and raised one eyebrow.

He shrugged. "So? I'm staying there for the rest of the week."

Kira nodded. "I see. Are we going to spend any time together while I'm here?"

"Listen, Kira—"

"Never mind." She shook her head. "It's not your fault I turned up unannounced. I just…" Tears filled her eyes, and she turned away, sniffling.

Dammit. Kira had only cried twice since they were kids, and both times had been due to traumatic events in her life. He dropped his bag and went to sit on the coffee table directly across from her. "What is it?"

She stared at him for a long moment, seemingly trying to decide if she was going to tell him whatever was on her mind. Then she took a deep breath and said, "I tried to make contact with my mother the day after I arrived here. It didn't go well."

"Okay." He frowned. What was going on with Kira and her parents? Even when they weren't getting along particularly well, they'd never stopped speaking to each other. "What didn't go well?"

"Everything." Tears flowed freely down her face now. "She… doesn't want to meet me."

Grayson shook his head, trying to clear the confusion. Did she have an event she wanted her mother to go to? It wouldn't be the first time her mother had declined an invitation. Kira's mom didn't really like the city or going to premieres. Too often Kira left her mother on her own while she networked with producers and directors. "Meet you where?"

"You don't understand," she said, shaking her head.

"I think that's pretty clear," he said. "What is it that's making you so upset?" He was really getting worried now. The woman sitting in front of him was one he didn't recognize.

She stared past him at the wall as she said, "There's something I never told you about my family."

He nodded once and then held his hand out to her. More tears spilled as she placed her hand in his. Then he waited, just holding on as he gave her the space she needed to get the words out. If there was one thing he knew about Kira, it was that she always did everything in her own time.

A clock on the wall ticked in the silence. Still, he waited.

Finally, she raised her gaze and held his as she said, "Right before we left for New York, I found out that I was adopted."

Grayson sucked in a breath, shocked by her admission. When he'd first told her he was leaving their hometown and his foster family behind, she mentioned something about going with him. But it had been sort of wistful, the kind of talk when someone wanted to do something but didn't really believe that they could. But then the day before he was set to leave, she'd crawled in his bedroom window. With tears in her eyes, she'd curled up with him in his bed and told him not to leave without her. She'd be on the bus with him. It was only the second time he'd ever seen her cry. At the time, he'd just thought she was emotional about leaving home or just didn't want him to leave without her.

Damn, he'd been naïve.

"Why didn't you tell me then? You could have, you know." There wasn't any accusation in Grayson's tone, only curiosity.

"I don't know." She closed her eyes as she ran a hand through her platinum hair. Then she said, "I was going to, but then I just couldn't. They told me in the heat of the moment, right after I told them I was going to New York with you. My mom used it as a weapon, accusing me of being ungrateful after all they did for me. My dad just sat there and let her rage at me. I guess once we got to New York, I just didn't want to think about it."

Grayson squeezed her hand, showing support in the only way he knew how. "You buried your pain."

She shrugged. "I guess you could say that. I was angry at

both of them, and then I started to romanticize meeting my birth mom."

"Did your parents know who she was?"

"No. Just that she was an actress."

The words hung in the air, and Grayson started to understand where all her determination came from to be the best. To always be on top. To appear perfect. To get a role that would put her in Oscar contention. His expression must have changed to one of understanding, because when he started to speak, she cut him off.

"Don't start psychoanalyzing me, Grayson."

"Okay," he said with a soft smile. "So you found out who she is?"

Kira nodded. "After…" She cleared her throat. "You know, after what happened a couple of years ago, I just couldn't stop thinking about her, so I hired a PI. It took all this time, but he finally got back to me."

"And you tried to contact her?"

"Yes, but when that didn't work, I had to get my lawyer involved because she wouldn't take my calls. He found out she wasn't interested in meeting or even talking to me." Her eyes filled with tears again, and she angrily wiped them away.

Grayson questioned her use of a lawyer to contact her birth mother, but considering Kira was a huge star, he supposed it made a certain amount of sense. She'd want someone else to make the initial phone call to make sure she wasn't walking into a public relations nightmare.

"The worst part is, the PI said she's known who I am for years. I guess that explains why I didn't get that part in *Last Year's Hope*." She let out a humorless laugh. "Talk about irony."

Grayson blinked at her, trying to put together what she'd just said. That movie, about a troubled relationship between a mother and her adult daughter, starred Jeanette Brooks, a legendary actress in Hollywood. "You mean… Jeanette Brooks is your—"

She slowly nodded.

"Holy shit."

"Yeah."

The implications of her confession were astounding. One of the most powerful actresses in Hollywood was her mother, had known Kira was her daughter, and still didn't want to meet her. Grayson's heart broke for her. "I'm so sorry, Kira."

"Me, too." She was full of sadness as she said, "I'm sorry for being such a bitch to Amelia at the café. I'd just found out about my mother, and I guess I went a little crazy. You're the only person in the world I can really talk to." She lowered her voice and whispered, "I guess I'm afraid I'll lose you."

"Kira," he said softly as he stood. "We are family. You're not going to lose me. Just because I need to make a life for myself that's different than yours, that doesn't mean I'm not your friend or that I won't be here for you." He tugged her to her feet and then wrapped her in his arms, holding her tightly. "You're my oldest and best friend. You know that."

"But Amelia needs you right now, and you're starting a family." Her voice trembled. "I just… I'm not sure where I fit into that."

"As Auntie Katy?" he asked hopefully. "I can't be the person who I used to be, the one who watched over all the stories and rumors. There are other PR people who can handle all of that just fine. But I can be the one you talk to when you need someone. The one who cheers you from the sidelines. And someone who never stops loving you no matter what."

She held onto him with everything she had, and after a moment, she said, "I'd really like that."

CHAPTER 19

By midafternoon, Amelia was restless. After surfing the internet, watching a movie, and then an hour of trying to concentrate on the book Grayson had left her, she was more than ready to get out of bed and actually do something. Anything. Yoga and baking were high on her priority list. She was so tired of sitting around, she'd even started daydreaming about cleaning out her freezer.

But she wasn't about to do anything that would put her child in danger. Instead, she grabbed her phone and scrolled through her contacts, looking for someone to chat with. She immediately ruled out Rex. He'd just annoy her with questions about Grayson, and if she told him about her fall, forget it. She'd never get rid of him. The man would be calling every few hours for an update.

She finally landed on Georgia's number, realizing she wasn't going to make it to the girls' night they'd planned. Besides, gossiping about Katy Carmichael didn't really hold much appeal anymore. There was too much history between her and Grayson. Amelia thought it better to just keep her mouth shut.

The phone rang four times before Georgia's voicemail picked up. Amelia left a quick message letting her know about the healer's orders and asking if they could reschedule a time to get together.

She was just about to call Yvette Townsend, the one person she'd known before she moved to town, when a news notification flashed on her phone.

The headline read: *Katy Carmichael in Love?*

If that was true, it really was news, Amelia thought. The actress hadn't said anything about dating anyone. In fact, at one point the night before, she'd even made a comment about how long it had been since she'd had a date with someone interesting. She'd laughed and jokingly referred to Grayson as the perfect man and said she should've never let him go all those years ago. It had been awkward and framed as a joke, but Katy hadn't exactly been shy about making sure Amelia knew that she thought of Grayson as hers and that Amelia was temporary.

Curious, Amelia opened the gossip column, and her eyes nearly bugged out when she spotted a photo of the actress wrapped in Grayson's arms. Her eyes were closed, while Grayson's were hidden by the way his head was bent in a way that made him look like he was going in for a kiss. She scanned the credits of the photo and let out a grunt of disgust when it was dated that same day.

Katy Carmichael was spotted in the small enchanted village of Keating Hollow just a few days ago. Sources say she's staying with her longtime friend and former employee Grayson Riley. It's been reported in the past that the pair have known each other since they were children, and there's speculation that they dated in the past. It appears that the couple are back on again, and a close source to Ms. Carmichael says, "She's happier than she's ever been." Looks like the Until There Was You *star is off the market.*

Amelia's stomach rolled and nausea made her queasy. She didn't pay much attention to the words of the short article. That appeared to be all speculation. Even the source they quoted was vague and likely missing context. It was the photo that made her uncomfortable. There was an intimacy to it that was hard to deny.

She took a closer look at the photo and determined that they'd been standing in Grayson's living room, near the front picture window. Clearly the paparazzi had taken it from outside without their knowledge.

Grayson had gone home that morning for a change of clothes and to pack a bag. Had he really gone home to see Katy? Amelia's mind kept filling with images of the two of them. And she kept hearing Katy's words when the woman had told her that Grayson would be back in New York soon. Had Grayson lied to her? Were they actually together, and was he just spending time with Amelia because of the baby?

Every insecurity Amelia had ever felt came roaring back, making her doubt herself and everything Grayson had said to her over the past few days.

It's just a picture, she told herself. And a gossip page story was more often wrong than right. Amelia knew Grayson deserved a chance to explain, that likely Grayson was just hugging his friend... But when she looked at it again, the nausea only intensified. That picture was not one that implied "just friends."

Amelia spent the next hour trying to put Grayson Riley and Katy Carmichael out of her mind. It didn't exactly work. She started to call Grayson numerous times, but stopped herself before completing any of the calls. This wasn't a conversation they should have over the phone. She wanted to see his facial expressions when she asked him about it. That didn't stop her from googling both Katy's and Grayson's names. She found one article from early on in Katy's career that connected her to him, but it didn't say anything other than she'd taken him to a premiere. There was nothing else other than a mention here and there about 'a statement made by Grayson Riley on Ms. Carmichael's behalf.' There was nothing scandalous, which made Amelia speculate that he'd been exceptionally good at his job.

A loud knocking on her door pulled Amelia out of her internet spiral. Grateful for a distraction, she got out of bed and went to answer it and found Georgia Exler on her doorstep. The author, who was wearing jeans, a thick sweater, and faux fur-lined boots, looked great with her dark curls framing her face.

"I guess you weren't kidding when you said you were on bedrest," Georgia said, smiling as she looked Amelia up and down.

Amelia glanced down at herself. She'd ditched her satin pajamas for a pair of soft leggings, thick wool socks, and an oversized sweatshirt with a wine stain on the left side. "Isn't this a standard stay-at-home outfit?"

"Sure, but most people comb their hair," she teased.

Amelia ran a hand through her locks and grimaced when she realized one side was all knotted up. But then she shrugged and let the other woman in. "I wasn't expecting company, so who cares, right?"

Georgia chuckled. "As a shut-in who sometimes goes days without seeing anyone, I fully understand. But get cleaned up. We have somewhere to be."

Amelia blinked at her. "Didn't you get my message? I'm not supposed to be on my feet." She glanced down at herself and sighed. If Grayson were there, he'd have already ordered her to sit down.

Grayson.

Her heart ached just thinking about him.

"I got it. But where we're going, you won't be on your feet at all. Just brush that hair of yours and put on a clean sweatshirt. Trust me." She grinned at Amelia. "You're in safe hands."

Amelia hesitated, unsure. She desperately wanted to get out of her house, but she wouldn't do anything that would put her pregnancy in danger. "Where are we going?"

"Faith's spa. It's closed for the evening, but Hanna convinced her to let us come have a girls' night with facials, mani-pedis, and sea scrubs. No massages for you because of your condition, but I bet you could talk someone into an eyebrow threading or various waxings if that's your thing."

Amelia pressed her fingers to her eyebrows, suddenly self-conscious. "Are my brows that bad?"

Georgia leaned in, studying Amelia. "No, but they probably could use a little shaping."

Nodding, Amelia made a snap decision and said, "Give me a few minutes."

It had been a at least a couple of months since Amelia had indulged in any self-care. And if there was ever a day that she needed it, this was the one. As long as she could sit back and relax, there was no harm in going to the spa.

∼

"You made it!" Hanna said, reaching out and hugging Amelia. The café owner held on for a little longer than was necessary, but Amelia didn't mind. After spending two full days holed up in her house, it was good to be with other women. Hanna released Amelia, said hello to Georgia, and then gestured for them to follow her. "Come on, let's get this party started." She led them out onto the spa's patio and gestured to the zero gravity chairs. "Sit here. Anything you want will be brought to you."

"Thanks." Amelia laid out in one of the chairs and glanced around the outdoor area of the spa. Even though the temperature in Keating Hollow was cold enough to make one's teeth chatter, the outdoor space of the spa was anything but cold. The zero gravity chairs were positioned in a circle around an impressive outdoor firepit, while other outdoor heaters were set up at various spots behind them, creating a warm cocoon. There were also twinkle lights illuminating the lush space that was filled with various plants and gorgeous flowers that were clearly out of season for their temperature zone.

The door leading into the spa opened and a petite woman with blond hair tied up in a flowing ponytail stepped out. Her green eyes were alight with joy as she glanced around at Hanna, Georgia, and then Amelia, who said, "You must have an earth witch on staff who keeps everything blooming."

Faith Townsend chuckled. "Not on staff. It's my dad. Now that he's basically handed over operations of the brewery to my brother-in-law Clay and Hanna's husband, Rhys, he's had a little time on his hands. He likes to stop by once a week or so and tend to the garden out here. Isn't it fantastic? Before he started managing it, all we had were soothing rocks and waterfalls."

"It's really lovely." Amelia felt so at peace there with the fire in front of her and the lavender blooming behind her.

"Lin, Faith's dad, is fantastic," Hanna said, leaning toward her. "He's sort of like the town's father figure. Willing to do anything for anyone, and he deeply cares about the town. We're lucky to have him."

"He sounds great," Amelia said, knowing that the Townsends were pretty much the heart of Keating Hollow, right along with the Pelshes. "Your dad seems pretty great, too. I met him at Shannon's wedding. He's really excited about turning the winery into something great for the town."

Hanna's expression softened. "Yeah, he is. How about you? I know Rex is your brother and is living in Christmas Grove. Is the rest of your family there, too?"

Amelia shook her head. "Nope. My mom, stepdad, and my stepmom and all my other half siblings are Back East. My dad passed when I was pretty young. I'm really only close to Rex."

Hanna reached over and squeezed her hand. "I'm sorry to hear that about your dad. And it's too bad your family is so far away. But don't worry. We're your family now." She winked at her. "After this inauguration, as soon as it's safe for you, you'll be forced to engage in golf cart races, racy romance book clubs, and wine tasting parties. Not to mention the weekly facials and pedicures."

"Golf cart races?" Amelia asked with one eyebrow raised. "Where and when do those happen? And are there prizes involved?"

Hanna and Faith chuckled while Georgia listened with interest.

Faith passed out cups of herbal tea and said, "They usually happen down by the river. When? Just whenever the girls get together. Abby has a cart and so does Wanda. As far as prizes go, the reward is the sweet taste of glory."

"That about sums it up," Hanna said. "We ride in teams, and everyone is allowed to use their magic in any way that can give them an advantage. The only rule is that there aren't really any rules."

Amelia stared at them, not sure if they were being completely serious, but then decided she didn't care. If there were golf cart races, she was down. "Sign me up. Well, after I pop this baby out. I don't want to do anything to risk having to be on bedrest again."

"What happened?" Faith asked.

"I slipped on the snowy steps. Healer Whipple has taken good care of me, though. I'm sure everything will be fine. I just need to take it easy until the turkey is done, I guess." She smiled at them, thoroughly enjoying her girl time.

"That's why we modified girls' night. To mitigate your stress after that story hit this afternoon," Hanna said.

Amelia winced. She hadn't wanted to talk about Grayson or Katy. In fact, during the time she'd been hanging out at the spa, she hadn't thought of either of them once. She supposed it was unavoidable when the person you were dating had their face plastered on gossip sites with a massive star.

Georgia and Faith both stared at Hanna with disapproving expressions.

"What?" Hanna asked. "Are we really just going to ignore the elephant in the room? I wanted Amelia to know we have her back. After the way that jerk Katy acted the other day at the café, our girlfriend deserves some reinforcements, right?"

"Of course she does," Faith said, patting her friend's arm. "But if I saw Hunter in a picture like that with his ex, I probably wouldn't want to talk about it with a group of women I'd just met." She turned to Amelia. "I'm sorry. We can drop this. Just tell Hanna to mind her own business. It's okay. She's used to it. I tell her that all the time."

"No you don't," Hanna said with a laugh.

"I would if I thought you were being nosey," Faith said with an air of indignation.

"Well, that's true enough. You're not one for holding back with anyone."

The pair of them chuckled while Georgia and Amelia looked on. Finally, Georgia turned to Amelia. "We're going to be besties like that one day."

"We are?" Amelia asked, grinning at her.

"Yep. I'm declaring it now, so expect me to start calling you all the time and meeting up for coffee dates."

"How often is all the time?" A lightness settled over Amelia that she hadn't felt in forever. It was that feeling of budding friendship that she hadn't allowed herself to really explore since she'd lost Victoria. Would she find what she'd been missing with Georgia? And if she did, would she allow herself to embrace it? She really hoped so, because after talking about Victoria with Grayson, it became clear to her that she couldn't continue to keep people at arm's length if she wanted to heal from that tragedy. The nightmares would just keep creeping up on her. But opening her heart again to friendship just might help her move on.

"Like once or twice a week. I'm a hermity writer. You can't expect too much," Georgia said with a smirk.

"Oh, good," Amelia said, relieved. "I'm not an everyday-phone-call kind of girl. I think this is going to work out just fine."

"Perfect." Georgia held her cup up to toast with Amelia. "It's a deal then. Girlfriends for life."

Amelia touched her mug to Georgia's and said, "Deal."

The other two cheered their approval.

"Who's ready for facials?" Faith asked, rising from her chair.

"Me!" the other three said in unison.

"On it. Let me get Esme and Lena. They're going to take care of us tonight." Just as Faith started to retreat into the building, Amelia's phone started to ring.

"Oh, sorry," Amelia said, fishing it out of her pocket. "I'll put it on silent—" She stared at the name flashing across the screen and then felt her nausea reemerge.

"What's wrong?" her new bestie asked. "Who is it?"

"Grayson," Amelia said, staring at the phone as if it were going to bite her.

"You can just not answer, you know," Georgia said. "You don't have to talk to him."

"I know. I just… I'm supposed to be at home, and I'm sure he's wondering where I am."

Georgia held her hand out for the phone. "Give it to me. I'll tell him for you."

Amelia shook her head. "No. You don't need to do that. I've got this." She pressed the Accept button.

Georgia leaned in and whispered, "If at any point you're over it, you can just give me the phone. Understand?"

With her lips curved into a half smile, Amelia nodded. Yeah, she could be besties with a woman like Georgia, one who respected her choices but always had her back. Was that what all adult friendships looked like? She didn't really know because she'd kept herself closed off for so long. It was definitely time to change that.

"Amelia? Hello?" Grayson asked.

"It's me." She stared at the fire, trying to sear that image of him and Katy out of her mind.

"Where are you?" he asked. "I'm worried about you."

"Out with friends," she said, deliberately not telling him the details. It was sort of petty, but she was still smarting from the article.

"What do you mean by 'out'? You're supposed to be on bedrest."

"I'm with Georgia and a couple of other ladies. Don't worry. I'm off my feet and taking care of the baby." Then she added, "You can go home. I'm sure you'd like to spend more time with Katy anyway."

He sighed. "No, I don't want to go home. I want to be here."

"Are you sure about that?" This time there was ice in her tone.

There was a long pause. "You saw that gossip article, didn't you?"

"Unfortunately." The ache in her stomach intensified, and she wondered if she was going to throw up.

"You know all of that is just speculation after a gross invasion of privacy. I'm not with her. You know that," he said softly.

"Maybe not, but that picture was from today, and you know what, Grayson? It's hard for photos to lie. You two looked far too intimate."

"That was nothing," he insisted. "She'd just finished telling me something important, and I was giving her a hug. Nothing more. I swear."

She didn't say anything. There wasn't anything to say. She knew what that picture made her feel, and none of it was good.

"You do believe me, don't you?"

"To be honest, I'm not sure." She just didn't know what she was supposed to think. Maybe being involved with a man who was so closely connected to someone else was a mistake.

"Dammit," he muttered. "Is there anything I can say to make you believe me? Because it sounds like you've already made up your mind."

"I just need some space, Grayson. Can you give me that? Go home, and we'll talk tomorrow."

There was silence over the line, and she started to wonder if he'd ended the call. But then he said, "All right. If that's what you need. Call me if… Well, just call me."

"Okay," she said softly and then pressed End. She closed her eyes and let out a groan because she wasn't entirely convinced that she wasn't making a mountain out of a molehill.

"Taking a step back to think is never a bad thing," Georgia said.

"She's right," Hanna agreed.

"Yep." Faith said.

Amelia opened her eyes and smiled gratefully at them. "Thank you."

"You're welcome," Faith said. "Now, about those facials. Are we ready?"

They all nodded enthusiastically, and from the moment Esme started cleaning her face, Amelia really did manage to put Grayson and Katy Carmichael out of her mind for the next few hours while the ladies who worked at the spa pampered her silly.

CHAPTER 20

*G*rayson paced his kitchen, frustrated beyond belief. He'd come home to a crowd of paparazzi hanging out on his front lawn. Flash bulbs had gone off in his face, followed by a dozen questions about his relationship with Katy Carmichael. He'd ignored their questions and done his best to try to get the photographers to move off the property. When they didn't listen, he'd had to make a call to Drew Baker, the town's deputy sheriff, to get them to move across the street.

Dealing with the paparazzi was something he'd become accustomed to over the years, but it was different when he was living in a small house on a regular residential street. There weren't any gates or security to keep them out. And it pissed him off.

At least they hadn't drawn a crowd of fans the way they often did in the city. It was the only consolation. He'd stepped into his house, and immediately went to work on closing all the blinds. He'd be damned if another picture of him or Kira showed up online.

He didn't blame Amelia for being skeptical about that story in the gossip rag. The picture really did make it look like Grayson and Kira were a couple. The irony was that after all the time they'd spent together, not one gossip rag had run a story about them before. He wondered why now.

He picked up his phone, and after scrolling through his contacts, he found the number he wanted and made a call. Ten minutes later, after a terse conversation with the legal department at the parent company of the gossip site, he got a verbal agreement that they'd take down the story. It was something he'd done countless times throughout his tenure as Katy Carmichael's public relations manager. In fact, he'd dealt with that particular lawyer before. The history often made things move along faster.

Movement in the hallway caught his attention, and he looked up to see Kira standing there and clutching her suitcase handle. He raised an eyebrow. "I didn't even realize you were here."

"I went out for coffee, but as soon as the story broke, I came back here. It was only a matter of time before the paps showed up."

He nodded. It was just a reality for her everyday life. He glanced at her suitcase. "You're leaving already?"

"I think I should. I've done too much damage here." She pressed her lips together in a thin line. "I don't want to mess up your life, Grayson. I just needed a safe space to land for a bit after everything that's happened. But now that the press has found me, they won't leave either of us alone while I'm here. We both know that."

He didn't move from his spot as he studied her. She was wearing jeans, a long-sleeved cotton shirt, and white Chucks.

Her hair was tied into a low ponytail on one side, and if she was wearing any make-up, he couldn't see it. The woman standing in front of him didn't look at all like Katy Carmichael. She looked like Kira, the girl he'd run off to New York with when they were just eighteen. On the one hand, he was relieved she was going back to New York. Without her there, the press wouldn't care what he was up to. And he was certain it would ease tensions with Amelia. On the other, he was worried about her and feared if she went back home she'd fall right back into her old patterns. "Are you sure that's what you want to do?"

"I'm sure." She nodded solemnly. "I'm a big girl, and I can't count on you to fix all of my problems for the rest of my life." Kira gave him a soft smile. "You've got a good thing going here with Amelia and the family you're going to start. It's not fair of me to mess that up for you."

It was strange to hear those words from her. For the past decade, she'd treated him like he belonged to her. As if he'd be forever by her side for the rest of their lives. Something had changed with her, but he wasn't exactly sure what. "What will you do when you get home?"

"The usual. Spend the day at the spa. Go shopping. Hang out at the club." She forced a smile, the one she always used when she was lying.

"Kira," he said. "Come on. Be honest. What's going on with you?"

"Nothing. I just…" She walked over to the table and sat down, gesturing for him to sit with her. Once he was seated, she leaned forward with her elbows on her knees and said, "I've been doing a lot of soul searching these past couple of days. Ever since I heard that my birth mom doesn't want to meet me, I've been questioning what I'm doing with my life. I think maybe I just need to go spend some time with myself, trying new things that don't involve acting or red carpets or photo shoots."

He reached out and squeezed her hand, glad that she was planning to take some time for herself. She'd been working nonstop for over a decade. It was about time she did something just for her. "I think that's a great idea. Will you do that in New York?"

She shook her head. "No. There's a house in Rhode Island that I've already put an offer on. It's on the coast but away from people in the industry, and it's available for me to move in immediately. I told my finance manager to put the Cape Cod house on the market. It's time to let that one go."

He nodded, understanding. The Cape Cod house was full of terrible memories for both of them. It wasn't a place to go to heal. "Text me the address so I'll know where to find you."

She grinned at him. "I already put it in your contacts."

"What?" He yanked his phone out, tapped in his passcode, and scrolled to her name. Sure enough, there was a Rhode Island address. "When did you do this?"

"This morning when you were in the shower." She got up, patted his knee, and said, "Benji is waiting outside. I'll call you when I'm settled in Rhode Island."

He rose and followed her to the door. "Kira?"

"Yeah?"

"There's something that's been bothering me," he said.

"What's that?"

"Where the hell has Benji been this whole time, and is he the one who's been driving you around town?"

"Yes. He's my driver. Who else?" When he just shrugged,

she continued. "He's been staying at the Keating Hollow Inn. When he wasn't there, he was exploring the town. His favorite place is A Spoon Full of Magic, the chocolate place near the café."

"Of course it is," Grayson said with a laugh. Her driver had the biggest sweet tooth he'd ever seen. "Tell him I said hello and that I'm sorry I missed him."

"Will do." She pulled the door open, turned to stare right at the paparazzi, waved and blew them a kiss, then hurried over to the black Town Car sitting in his driveway. Benji opened the door for her, grabbed her suitcase and stored it in the trunk before taking his place behind the wheel. By the time the car disappeared around the corner, all of the photographers were already dispersing. It looked like his days of dealing with paparazzi had come to an end.

Grayson shook his head, grabbed his keys, and headed for the Keating Hollow Brewery. The place was certainly quieter than it had been the last time he'd been there. This time Rhys was the only one behind the bar. Grayson slid onto a barstool and waited patiently for him to finish pouring someone else a beer.

"Hey, man," Rhys said jovially. "I thought for sure you'd have your hands full tonight after that story broke."

Groaning, Grayson rubbed a hand over his face. "They probably would've been if Amelia hadn't canceled on me and Katy hadn't left town."

"Damn. That sounds rough. So you lost them both in one day?" Rhys had that concerned tone that most bartenders had managed to perfect.

"I didn't lose, Katy. She's just a friend who showed up for a few days and then went home. Amelia?" He gritted his teeth as he thought about their last phone call. "I have no idea. But I guess I can't blame her if she doesn't want to sign up to spend time with a guy who sometimes ends up in the tabloids because of his association with a famous actress. No one wants that drama."

"But isn't Amelia having your child?" Rhys asked, leaning forward on the bar.

"Yep. That's the real bitch of it." He glanced at the taps. "Can I get a beer? Something dark."

"Of course." Rhys moved over to the taps and went to work. "Listen, I know you're worried about Amelia, but something tells me it's all going to work out. So just hang in there, okay?"

"Why do you say that? Do you even know Amelia?" Grayson asked.

"Sure. She's come in here, and I've seen her around Hanna's café quite a bit. She and Hanna have formed a friendship. In fact, aren't they together right now at Faith's spa?"

Grayson nodded. He was glad to hear she was making friends. She deserved to have that in her life. "Yeah. She said it was girls' night."

Rhys nodded. "Right. Let's just hope they don't get the golf carts out." His smile grew into a grin. "On a night like tonight, that would be a lot of mud to deal with later."

"Do I even want to know what you're talking about?" he asked.

"Probably not. Well, not unless you like stripping your girl down and washing the mud out of her hair."

Grayson would gladly do that and more. But mud in her hair? He narrowed his eyes at the other man. "I think you need to tell me more."

He threw his head back and laughed. "It's not the kind of

thing you explain. It's more of an adventure you need to experience. Hold on. Let me call Clay."

Grayson waited as Rhys made the call. A few minutes later, Rhys grinned at him and said, "Better finish that beer. The party will be here shortly."

CHAPTER 21

Amelia couldn't remember a time when she'd been more relaxed. Her time at the spa with her new circle of friends had been everything she'd never known she needed. Her toes were sparkly, her brows were shaped, and her skin was radiant. She made a mental note to start scheduling self-care days at least once a month. She deserved it, right? Of course she did.

"Hey, ladies," Hanna called as she walked back out onto the patio holding a tray of cookies. "Better get a snack, because it looks like our night isn't over yet."

Amelia took one of the pink frosted sugar cookies, and couldn't deny that she felt like a little girl on Christmas. This girls' night was the gift that kept on giving. "What's next? Body scrubs from Hotties R Us?"

Georgia snickered. "Now that would be one hell of a service. What do you say, Faith? When can I book my appointment?"

"Uh, excuse me, but as the bestie, I think I'm entitled to priority status," Hanna said as she batted her eyelashes at Faith.

Faith rolled her eyes. "I'm pretty sure that kind of service would involve a very different kind of business permit."

"We can probably fundraise for the fee." Hanna gave her an innocent smile.

"I bet you could. I wonder what Rhys would think about that?"

Hanna flipped her dark curls over her shoulder and let out a huff. "Please. He's working so much these days I'd half expect him to make the appointment for me himself just so he could get a little extra sleep... if you know what I mean."

Faith laughed.

Georgia let out a sigh. "I *wish* I knew what you meant. It's been way too long since this girl has had anything from Hotties R Us."

"Me, too," Amelia said.

All three of the other women turned and stared first at her and then her belly.

Amelia's face warmed. She cleared her throat and added, "Well, at least a few months anyway."

"Seriously?" Georgia said. "You haven't been getting it on with that hot man? Not even while he's been staying with you?"

She shook her head. "Nope. We just reconnected and are sort of taking it slow."

"Sort of is one way of putting it," Georgia teased.

"Okay, Hanna," Faith said, her eyes twinkling with amusement. "What is it you have planned for us next? A trip to the brewery so you can get a quickie in the office with your hubby?"

"Funny," Hanna deadpanned at the petite blonde. "Like you and Hunter haven't christened a few spaces here at the spa."

Faith made a non-committal shrug. "This girl doesn't kiss and tell."

"Sure she doesn't." Hanna turned to Georgia and Amelia. "Anyway, come on. We're off on the next adventure."

Georgia popped up out of her zero-gravity chair, but Amelia took her time, not wanting to miss out but also knowing she should go home. Being at the spa had been fine, but she'd been waited on hand and foot the entire time. If they were going out… that was against Healer Whipple's orders. She wasn't about to disobey.

Still, Amelia followed them into the spa and out into the reception area. "Guys?"

All three of them turned to look at her.

"This has been really great, but I think I better get home. I'm just not supposed to be on my feet much and—"

The door swung open, making the bells chime, and four handsome men walked in, all smiles and their expressions full of mischief. But there was one in particular that drew Amelia's attention. "Grayson?" she asked. "What are you doing here?"

He walked over to her and slipped his hand over hers, squeezing gently. Then he pulled her away from the rest of the group and lowered his voice. "I know you said you needed a little space, and I fully intended to give it to you. I swear."

"And yet, you're here," she said, cocking an eyebrow.

"It appears so." He glanced back at the other guys. Rhys had his arm around Hanna while Clay stood nearby talking to Georgia. There was a guy she didn't recognize with his arm around Faith, who, she assumed, was her husband, Hunter.

"Is this some sort of double date on steroids?" Amelia asked him.

He chuckled. "It sure looks like that, doesn't it?"

"Uh-huh."

"No. Not a date at all. Golf cart races." He grinned at her. "I got dragged along by Rhys, not even knowing we were going to come here. Though, I can't say I'm unhappy about it."

Her heart sank as she stared at him and then the rest of the crowd. She'd heard a lot about the infamous golf cart races, but she couldn't participate. What had Grayson been thinking? "That'll probably be fun for you, but we both know I can't do this. I'm going to head home. I shouldn't even be on my feet now."

"I know," Grayson said quickly. "That's why we aren't racing. We're the judges."

"So you think I'm just going to stand around while other people race in golf carts?" she asked, sounding exasperated.

"No. They brought us a third cart to use." He tugged gently at her hand. "Just come check it out, and then if you still want to go home, I'll take you."

She sighed. "All right. But just for a minute. I've already been on my feet too long."

Grayson led the way, and once they were outside the building, she spotted three golf carts. One was purple, decked out with flashing lights, and sat six people. Prince's "1999" blared from the speakers, and Wanda Danvers, the real estate agent who'd helped her find her rental, sat behind the wheel talking animatedly into the phone. "You're missing out, Abby. I'm telling you it's going to be epic," she said as she waved at Amelia. Amelia waved back, smiling at the other woman.

A second six-person cart without any obvious alterations was parked right next to Wanda's. And the last one was a four-seater with oversized tires and custom seats that looked like they were designed for the cab of a truck, not a golf cart.

"That last one is ours," Grayson said. "It's Lincoln

Townsend's. He had it modified to be more comfortable a few months back because he uses it a lot at his orchard."

Amelia walked over to the cart in question, staring at it wide-eyed. "I can't believe this. It looks a lot more comfortable than those other two."

"It is. I was the one who drove it over here." He gestured to the back where there was a pillow and a blanket. "Those are for you just in case you get cold or need more back support."

The door of the spa opened, and the rest of the gang filed out.

"Hey, Amelia," Hanna called. "You in?"

Amelia took a moment to consider, and as she glanced around at everyone, a smile curved her lips. "Yeah, I'm in. Let's do this."

"Yes!" Georgia said, running up to her and giving her a quick hug. "Make sure you declare my team the winner. It's a bestie's duty. You know that, right?"

"I'm on it," Amelia said, saluting her. "Now, go make it look good at least. If you're way behind, I'll still call it for you, but you know, they might notice it's rigged."

She chuckled. "I'll make sure not to disappoint you." With a wave, she ran over to the purple cart and jumped into the front seat next to Wanda. The pair seemed to know each other already and almost immediately started laughing at something one of them had said.

In no time, the women filled Wanda's cart and the three men took the other cart. Grayson helped Amelia into their ride, and then Grayson drove, following the racers down Main Street toward the river. Music was still playing, and Amelia started to feel like a carefree teenager again. She smiled at Grayson and said, "Thank you. Even just tooling around is fun."

He returned her smile and then offered his hand. She hesitated for a moment but then slipped her fingers between his. Grayson held her hand right up until he had to make a right turn onto the dedicated golf cart path that ran through town.

"This is pretty cool," Grayson said. "I had no idea this was here."

"I did. When I first came to town, I spent a lot of time walking around just to think stuff through. This path was a nice surprise. I didn't know about the golf cart races until very recently though, and I haven't been in one either."

Grayson chuckled. "I guess it's a good thing we're just the judges. Less pressure."

"Yeah." Amelia pressed her palm to her belly. "Not until this peanut shows up."

Grayson's expression turned soft as he nodded his agreement. "No argument here."

The other two golf carts came to a stop not far from the river's edge. Grayson maneuvered their cart until they were parked off to the side as observers.

Both Hanna and Rhys jumped out of the carts. They stood with their heads together, clearly debating something. When they were done, they shook hands and then turned to their respective teams.

"Rhys and I have agreed," Hanna said. "Since we have judges this time, we've decided the race will be determined entirely on the basis of technique. It doesn't matter who crosses the finish line first. The only thing we care about is magical style. Whichever team has the most flair will be declared the winner."

"Sweet!" Wanda, who was standing next to her cart, raised her arms in the air and swiveled her hips. "I'm all about the style." Georgia and Faith jumped out and mimicked her. Faith put a little too much juice into her swivel and toppled over right into a small patch of mud. When she sat up, a clump of it was caught in her hair.

"Dammit!" Faith said just as everyone else fell out laughing.

When the hysterics started to die down, Rhys pointed at Faith and then called to Grayson. "See? Mud. Every time."

Grayson nodded at him and said, "I look forward to the cleanup."

Rhys nodded with a knowing smile.

"What's that all about?" Amelia asked.

Grayson just chuckled. "Nothing important."

"Right." Amelia eyed him, thoroughly enjoying herself. She knew she was supposed to be taking time to figure out how she felt about dating a man who appeared to still be emotionally tied to someone else, but she just didn't want to think about anything other than having a good time.

"Amelia," Hanna said, striding toward her. "Like we talked about before, there aren't really any rules. We're still going to race to the end and back, but just look at what we do magically, and then you and Grayson decide the winner. The prize is bragging rights, so really, no pressure."

"That's what you think," she said, nodding toward Georgia. "She's already ordered me to declare her the winner. Everyone better bring something special, or else they're doomed."

Hanna just rolled her eyes and hurried back over to her cart. "Girls versus boys. Let the revelry begin!"

There was no hesitation. Both carts took off at full speed. The women's cart had a rain cloud right over it, giving off a torrential amount of rain as well as some thunder. The men's cart had mud all over the windshield from the constant barrage of mud balls flying at it.

Other shenanigans ensued as each group tried to slow the other one down, and Amelia had to wonder if they'd forgotten that crossing the finish line first didn't necessarily make them the winner.

But when Wanda started making tiny fire-breathing dragons swoop around the carts, that's when things got wild. Flying water monkeys, mud trolls, a flock of leaves in the shape of birds, and a variety of other animated animals appeared. At first, they seemed to be avoiding the other side, but the minute they collided, that was the ballgame. Small fire-breathing mud monkeys started running around the carts, making Amelia laugh.

Finally Amelia blew a special whistle and said, "I've seen enough. The prize goes to... the women's cart! The only reason you won is because I loved Wanda's use of mixed media."

The guys groaned while the women cheered and slapped hands. "Winners!" they cried out together.

"At least we have mud," Rhys said as he walked past them and hugged Hanna from behind.

"What's so great about mud?" Amelia asked.

"The cleanup is fun for some people," Grayson said.

"If you say so." Amelia leaned back in the bench seat and said, "I wish we could stay longer, but I'm starting to get really tired."

"Okay, let's go." Grayson got back behind the wheel, and after they said goodbye to their new friends, they took off back toward town.

"You're going to take me home on this?" Amelia exclaimed. Was he nuts? She lived halfway up the mountain.

"No." He rolled his eyes at her. "We're taking it back to Lin and then we'll pick up my SUV. I left it there."

"Oh, good," she let out a sigh of relief. "I was afraid I'd be frozen by the time we got there."

He glanced over at her and shook his head. "Have I ever not taken care of you?"

She shook her head. "Nope."

"That's what I thought. Now relax. I'll have you home in no time."

"Grayson?" she asked.

"Yeah?"

"Thank you," she said softly. "I had a really nice time tonight."

"So did I."

"When we get back to my place, do you think we can talk?" Amelia asked, her chest aching because she didn't want to talk about the story that came out earlier that day, but they really had no choice.

"Are you sure you're up for it tonight?" he asked. "I know you're tired."

"Not that tired." She hadn't stopped looking at him all night, and suddenly she wished she wasn't on bedrest. Because all she wanted was to wrap her arms around him and make him hers again.

CHAPTER 22

Grayson followed Amelia into her house and said, "Go make yourself comfortable. I'll make us some hot chocolate."

She smiled at him, that warm smile he'd come to take so much comfort in. "Thanks." After giving him a quick kiss on the cheek, she disappeared down the hall with Grayson watching her.

Hope bloomed deep in his chest. All night she'd been relaxed and happy. That had to mean good things, right? Maybe with Kira gone they could put that damn story behind them and get back to where they'd been, ready to try again.

He busied himself in the kitchen, and when he returned to the living room, Amelia was already curled up on the couch with a blanket wrapped around her legs.

"Thank you." She smiled up at him and cupped both palms around the mug.

"Anytime." He took a seat at the other end of the couch and said, "I want to apologize for that picture on that website this morning."

She tilted her head and asked, "Just that it was published, that I saw it, or for the content itself?"

There wasn't any accusation in her tone, just a mild curiosity. He cleared his throat. "All three, I guess? The story is garbage, and I was able to get them to take it down already."

"You did? Wow. I guess you really were good at your job." There was a hint of a teasing smile on her lips.

He let out a soft chuckle. "I had to be if I wanted to stay employed in that kind of work for any length of time."

"I guess so." She took a sip of her hot chocolate and let out a tiny moan of pleasure.

Damn, he wanted to hear that again. But the next time, he wanted it to be his lips on hers that elicited that sound. "As for the content, I wasn't kissing her. I was hugging her after she told me something really painful and personal. I know how it looks, but I swear it isn't that."

She nodded. "Honestly, I think I already knew that."

"Really? How?" He was desperately curious to know why she'd decided to trust him. He wasn't sure he deserved it. Not after the way he'd left her back in December.

"When I was relaxing at the spa, I had time to think about the last few days. It occurred to me that you spent very little time with Katy, instead, choosing to stay here with me and take care of my every need. You weren't desperate to spend any time with her. And when she was here, your interactions with each other were familiar, comfortable, but not indicative of two people who seemed romantically interested in one another. More like brother and sister, even though I know you *used* to be a couple."

"Yeah. I'd say that's pretty accurate. We certainly fight like brother and sister often enough," he said, nodding his agreement. "I honestly don't see her in a romantic way anymore. Besides, that relationship was more about each of us needing someone than being some great love match. We broke it off, and that was that. We've never been together again after that."

"You stuck around because you're a caregiver," she said and reached for his hand. "You have a need to take care of the people around you."

He couldn't deny that. His therapist had once told him it was likely a byproduct of losing his parents at such a young age. He had a deep-seated desire to protect those he loved. "Guilty."

"I also realized that the one thing you've never done is lie to me. Did you hold stuff back? Sure. But now that I know why, I completely understand. So why did I let one stupid gossip article come between us? Pure jealousy and insecurity."

"You don't have anything to be insecure about." He caressed her cheek. "I'm in love with you."

Emotion flickered through her eyes. "I believe you. But doubt definitely creeped in when I saw that picture. I know what she means to you. And I'm okay with it. But I think sometimes I'm going to have to work through my own abandonment issues and not put them on you when I see stuff like that. Because I love you, too, and I'll admit that I'm afraid to lose you again."

He slid closer to her and pulled her into his arms. "You're not going to lose me," he whispered.

She didn't say anything, just buried her face into his shoulder and held on. Still, there was something about the way she'd stiffened slightly that bothered him. She still didn't fully believe that he was hers. All he could do was keep on proving himself day in and day out. It might take some time, but he was determined, and patience was something he had to spare.

"Come on," he said, rising from the couch. "It's late. Let's get you and that baby of ours to bed."

She didn't resist as he tugged her to her feet, and when they got to her bedroom, she turned to him and slowly started to unbutton his shirt.

Grayson stood still, watching her take her time undressing him. It wasn't until she'd shoved his shirt all the way off and placed her hands on his chest that he let out a small sigh of pleasure. "I've missed you touching me."

"Me, too." She leaned in and kissed him slowly before reaching for the button of his jeans. It wasn't long before she had him just in his boxer briefs. Every nerve was on fire for her. It had been way too long since they'd been together, and even though he knew they wouldn't be taking things too far that evening, he still reveled in her touch. It was enough to just be near her like this. The rest could wait.

"My turn," he said, tugging on her sweater and lifting it over her head. She stood there in just her black lace bra and leggings, her small bump mesmerizing him. Sliding his hands to her hips, he lowered himself to his knees and placed a kiss on her belly, worshiping her and everything she'd brought into his life. "You're perfect in every way, Amelia."

She let out a tiny whimper and buried her hands in his hair as he continued to rain kisses all over her skin.

"These need to go," he said, tugging at her leggings.

Amelia nodded and watched him as he stripped her of the rest of her clothes, leaving her completely bare.

Grayson sucked in a sharp breath at her beauty. She was radiant, full of love and life and everything good. "I just want to lie skin to skin with you tonight and to worship you with my hands and lips."

Trembling, Amelia nodded and relieved him of the briefs that had kept him restrained.

After cupping both of her cheeks and kissing her thoroughly, Grayson took her by the hand and tugged her into the bed where they spent the rest of the night exploring each other with hands and lips but stopping short of doing anything that would risk her pregnancy. It was both tortuous to hold himself back and, at the same time, beautiful the way they cared for one another, showing their love through soft touches and tender kisses. There'd be time for more later, but for now, spending the night in her arms, showing her just how much he loved her, was enough.

~

IN THE DAYS THAT FOLLOWED, Grayson all but formally moved into Amelia's house. He still had his rental in town but never went there unless he needed to pick something up. Life was entirely domestic, and he thought he'd never been happier.

Grayson had just finished making dinner when he heard the door open. He smiled to himself and poured Amelia a glass of ginger ale. It was a new craving for her along with strawberries. It seemed she could never get enough of either these days.

"Dinner's ready in five," he called out.

"Can it wait?" she asked from behind him.

He smiled at her over his shoulder. "It's salad and lasagna, so it's nothing that is going to spoil too quickly. Why?"

She slipped her arms around him and pressed a kiss to his neck before whispering, "Healer Whipple gave me good news. Since there's been no more bleeding and my back is feeling better, she said there aren't any more restrictions. No more bedrest. I can go back to work as long as I don't engage in any heavy lifting, and…" Amelia nipped at his neck right below his ear. "We're in the clear for bedroom activities."

Grayson turned in her arms and smirked at her when he said, "So, Monopoly and Backgammon?"

She chuckled. "Only if we play strip Monopoly and Backgammon."

He grinned at her, reached back to turn off the oven, and then pulled her down the hall to the bedroom. "It looks like we have some catching up to do."

Giggling, she fell onto the bed with him. In no time, their clothes were on the floor and Amelia was lying under him with her limbs wrapped around his body.

"Damn, I'm going to enjoy this," he said, lowering his head to press a kiss to the swell of her breast.

"You damn well better," she breathed and arched her back, pressing herself against him. "Otherwise, we're gonna have some issues."

"No issues here," he said. And then he went to work, making her moan with pleasure over and over and over again until deep into the night.

CHAPTER 23

"She lives!" Georgia cried and threw her arms open wide for Amelia when she walked into Incantation Café.

Amelia grinned at her friend and embraced her with a hug. "Sorry! It's been a busy few weeks."

"Sure it has." Hanna rolled her eyes and set three coffee cups on the table next to a couple of pastries. "Being holed up in that house with Grayson must've been just torture for you."

Flushing, Amelia averted her gaze. She and Grayson really had been MIA when it came to polite society. After the night with the gang on the golf carts, they'd spent the majority of their time at her house. They'd even missed the barbeque at Lin Townsend's home because Amelia was still technically on bedrest and had a little bit of nausea to deal with. "I am back at work now, you know."

"Uh-huh. I heard part-time." Georgia winked at her.

Amelia just shrugged. Since she'd told her boss that she wanted to be put on administrative duty until she gave birth, they'd complied, but there just wasn't that much work for her to do. She was fine with the part-time status. "I'm here now."

"Yes, you are." Georgia sat at the table and leaned forward, whispering, "And we want all the details."

"Yeah. Spill." Hanna grinned at her. "Some of us need to live vicariously through our friends who are still in the honeymoon phase."

Georgia rolled her eyes at Hanna. "Please, girlfriend. You just told me that Rhys kept you up half the night last night. I know you weren't talking about baking cookies."

Hanna laughed. "That doesn't mean I don't still want details. Besides, why are you discouraging her? You surely could use a refresher on what to do should a hottie get his paws on you."

The two bantered some more about Amelia's sex life while she sat back and sipped her decaf latte. When they finally turned to her with interested expressions, she said, "I'm still the type of girl who doesn't kiss and tell. But nice try."

"Nice hickey," Hanna said.

Amelia pressed her hand to her neck, wondering how the hell she'd missed the fact that Grayson had given her hickey. "Oh my gods, really?"

"No, not really." Hanna sat back in her chair, chuckling to herself. "But now we know it's possible."

Georgia shook her head at their friend. "Seriously? Since when have you become so thirsty for details of other people's private lives?"

She shrugged. "I don't know. But you're right; it is kinda new for me."

"Your clock must be ticking," Georgia said.

"Bite your tongue." Hanna physically recoiled, making Amelia laugh.

"You two are too much," Amelia said.

"That's probably true." Georgia took a sip of her coffee and said, "Let's get down to business. When's our next spa night?"

The three of them made plans to get together again soon and then moved on to Keating Hollow gossip. The word was that Silas's movie was being buzzed as Oscar worthy and that Shannon was busier than ever with trying to manage his career. Amelia wondered what that meant for his relationship with Levi and hoped they were finding a way to make things work.

"Did you hear that Gideon is buying the Enchanted K gallery?" Hanna asked.

"Miranda Moon's partner, Gideon?" Amelia asked, remembering that he already worked at the gallery. She knew Miranda was busy writing books and also screenplays with Cameron Copeland, and that Gideon was a former Hollywood producer. She got the impression that money wasn't exactly an issue with them.

"Yeah," Hanna said. "He's an artist now, so I guess that makes sense. The owner died recently and left it to her granddaughter, but it appears she doesn't really have time for it and wanted to sell it to someone she knew wouldn't turn it into something cheesy like a paint your own ceramics studio or something like that."

"Well, that's cool. I can't wait to go by there and see what new stuff he does with it," Amelia said, checking the time. She was supposed to meet Grayson for dinner. As soon as she picked up her phone, it started to ring. She didn't recognize the out-of-state number and didn't answer. When the voicemail popped up, she checked the transcription and paled.

It was a reporter trying to get a comment on a story. She

got up without a word and went outside to listen to the recording.

Hello, Ms. Holiday. This is Rosy Tester from the Hollywood Scene. *I'm calling to get a comment on a story we're about to run involving Katy Carmichael, Grayson Riley, and yourself. Please call back at your earliest convenience.*

Amelia hated the thought of talking to a reporter, but she needed to know what the story was about. She hit Call and waited while the phone rang and rang and rang, until finally someone picked up.

"Rosy Tester here. I assume this is Ms. Holiday?" the woman said.

Amelia nodded even though the woman couldn't see her. "It is. What's the story you're running?"

"Thank you for your quick reply. I'd like a comment on our story if you're willing."

"I think that entirely depends on what you're printing," Amelia said, already annoyed.

"Did you know your partner Grayson Riley was in a relationship with Katy Carmichael?" the reporter asked.

"I'm not sure why that's relevant to anything at all," Amelia said.

"It's relevant because we here at *Hollywood Scene* have been given reliable information that two years ago Katy Carmichael had an abortion, and sources say that Grayson Riley was the father. That Grayson forced her to have the abortion and then left her when she begged to try again. Were you aware of these events? And if so, how do you reconcile having a child with him now?"

Amelia's entire body went numb. This wasn't happening. It couldn't be. Her hand started to tremble, and the phone slipped from her grip, landing on the cobblestone sidewalk of Main Street.

"Whoa. Are you all right?" Shannon Ansell-Knox asked, appearing out of nowhere and picking up her phone. Amelia had heard that she and Brian were back from their honeymoon, but this was the first time Amelia had run into her.

Amelia stared at the auburn-haired beauty and shook her head. "No. There's a terrible news story about to break and they want me to comment on it."

"About you?" She handed Amelia her phone back and clutched her hand as she frowned.

"Mostly about Grayson and Katy Carmichael. But yes, they have me in there, too, I think."

Shannon muttered a curse. "I heard that Katy had been in town. Did something happen while she was here?"

"No." Amelia shook her head. "This is apparently from a few years ago, but it's highly personal and if they run it, it's going to be devastating to her. I really need to get home and talk to Grayson." Amelia turned and started hurrying toward her car.

"Wait," Shannon said, concern in her voice.

Amelia paused and glanced back at her.

She produced a card and handed it to Amelia. "I have a lot of contacts in the industry and the media. If I can help in any way, let me know. I'm sure Katy has lawyers who will work on things from her end, but if you or Grayson need help, I'll do what I can."

Amelia had no idea what that would be, and she had every confidence that Grayson would know what to do, but she appreciated Shannon's kindness. "Thank you. I'll call if something comes up." She started to rush to her car again, but right before she pulled her door open, she called, "Shannon?"

"Yeah?" the other woman said with her hand on the café door.

"Can you tell Georgia and Hanna I had to go and that I'll call them later?"

"Absolutely."

With a nod, Amelia climbed into her car and took off toward the mountain road that would lead her to Grayson.

Amelia let out a sigh of relief when she spotted the Toyota Highlander in her driveway. She'd try to call using her Bluetooth on the way, but Grayson hadn't picked up. She was afraid he'd still been out meeting with a client or stuck in an area with bad cell reception. If there was one thing Grayson never did, it was ignore Amelia's calls.

She rushed into the house. "Grayson?"

There were footsteps in the hallway, and she turned to find him standing there with his suitcase handle in one hand and his phone in the other. She stared at the phone, spotting the mobile airline ticket. A chill ran through her. This was Holly's vision playing out in front of her. Her brother's girlfriend had been one hundred percent correct when she'd said Amelia didn't like it one bit. "Going somewhere?"

"We need to talk," he said, setting down his suitcase and moving to her side.

She took a step back, needing a little bit of distance. She hadn't known what to think when she got the call from the reporter. Abortion? Grayson's baby? That all seemed highly unlikely considering how Grayson felt about having a child, but what if that was the real reason he'd left her in December?

"Amelia," he said, concern flooding his dark eyes. "What is it? Did the reporter call you, too?"

She nodded slowly and then sank down into the oversized chair.

Grayson let out a string of curses and dropped down onto the couch, rubbing at his neck with one hand as he spat out, "Those vultures."

"Where are you going?" Amelia tried again, staring at his suitcase where he'd left it at the end of the hall.

"Rhode Island. That's where Kira and her lawyers are. I need to do damage control. This isn't just Kira. It's you and me, too. My history, all of it, including my parents' accident. There's stuff in there about you and Victoria, too."

"Me and Victoria?" Amelia said with a gasp. "Why? That was eighteen years ago. Why would anyone bring that up?"

"Because pain sells. It's what they do. I imagine there is some article out there that detailed the fact that you were with her that day, so they ran with it even though it has nothing to do with Kira or the story they want to write. Whoever wrote this article, did some serious deep dives on all of our histories. And babe, I will do anything to keep this out of the media and keep those reporters away from you."

Tears stung the back of her eyes, but she blinked them back. This wasn't the time to break down. She didn't want to focus on the article or the painful memories it would invoke. Instead, she focused on Holly's vision. "Rhode Island? I thought you'd be headed to New York." That's what Holly had said, wasn't it? That in her vision he was holding a ticket to New York City?

"What?" His brow crinkled in confusion. "Why are you asking me that?"

"Holly told me she had a vision that you'd be holding a ticket to go to New York City." She grabbed his phone that was sitting on the coffee table and held the phone up, waiting for him to put in the password. He did without comment. When she opened the phone, there it was. The ticket to New York. "I thought you said Rhode Island?"

"NYC is the layover." He bit his lower lip. "Holly had a vision? You didn't tell me that."

She shrugged. "I try not to put too much stock in them, especially when they are of something I don't like. They usually lack context."

He nodded. "True. But I'm sorry this one came true. And I'm really sorry you're caught up in this. What did the reporter say to you?"

She recapped the conversation and ended with, "I didn't say anything. To be honest, I had no idea what to say."

"Listen, Amelia." He grabbed her hand, holding it with both of his. "Kira was pregnant. But she didn't have an abortion. She lost the baby. And then she needed a D & C. And no, I was definitely not the father. I swear."

Relief rushed through her, and she felt her entire body sag with relief. She'd hoped there was an explanation, but the shock of the reporter's words had left her completely rattled. As she sat there, staring at Grayson, all of her relief suddenly turned to immense sadness for Katy. "She lost the baby? That's horrible."

"It was. What's worse is that it happened during a time when I wasn't there. She called, but I ignored her because I was pissed at her behavior. I'd been trying to go off on my own, and she kept calling for trivial stuff. I'd had enough. Then this happened. It was fairly early on, and Kira didn't want to deal with the emergency room, so she stayed home and went through it by herself. It took until the next morning for her PA to finally track me down and beg me to go to her. She was a complete mess. By that evening she was in pain and it was clear she needed medical attention. I'm the one took her to the hospital and was with her when she had her D & C. It was awful and traumatic. If this gets out, it will wreck her."

"And you. It's not right of them to put your story in the magazine. You're not a public figure," she said, her heart aching that he'd have to relive that awful night.

"I'm pissed as hell, but it won't wreck me. I'm more worried about burying the story to protect both you and Kira."

This time tears did start to fall, but not because she was worried about herself. She realized she was completely and utterly in love with the man sitting across from her. He really was the protector she knew him to be. She was proud of him but also sad that he was leaving, and she had no idea when he'd be back.

"What is it, love?" he said softly. "What can I do to help?"

"I'll just miss you, that's all." She sniffed.

"Miss me?" he asked, confusion lining his face. "Oh. I guess I forgot to tell you. I got you a ticket, too. I'd like you to come with me."

Her mouth dropped open in pure shock. "You're serious?"

He nodded. "This affects you, too, right? No reason to stay behind unless you can't get the time off work."

"I can," she said immediately. With her being on administrative duty, she wasn't exactly essential. "When do we leave?"

He glanced at the clock on the wall. "Twenty-five minutes."

"I'll be ready."

CHAPTER 24

*G*rayson held Amelia's hand as they walked up to the gorgeous home on the bluff overlooking the Atlantic Ocean. He had to admit that he wouldn't have guessed that this would be a place Kira would've purchased. It was clearly a gorgeous house, but it was more traditional compared to the other places she'd purchased in the past. It had a much quieter elegance than the Cape Cod house or any of her homes in LA, New York, or Vail.

"This is amazing," Amelia said, glancing around at the grounds.

Grayson guessed the place was on about an acre of land. It was secured by a locked gate, but most of it was covered in green foliage, giving it more of an *Anne of Green Gables* feel. "It is pretty. Not what I expected at all."

"Me either to be honest," Amelia said. "Your friend seems like she'd prefer something more modern and sleeker than this."

"She usually does." He shrugged and rang the doorbell.

The door was opened immediately by Kira's longtime

house manager, Lindsey Crane. "Grayson. Thank goodness you're here." She waved him in but paused when she spotted Amelia. After clearing her throat, she asked, "And who might this be?"

"Lindsey, this is Amelia Holiday, my girlfriend and the other person the article mentioned."

"Nice to meet you," Amelia said, holding her hand out.

The house manager seemed nonplussed, but eventually shook Amelia's hand. "Yes. The pleasure is mine." She turned to Grayson. "Does Katy know she's coming?"

Grayson shrugged. "Does it matter?" Lindsey had known him for years. She knew damned well he'd never bring over anyone who was a threat to Kira.

"I suppose not. There's a mess to fix, and I reckon you're the only one who can get it done at this point." She stepped aside, and Grayson and Amelia entered the newly remodeled home.

Grayson glanced around and wondered who'd decorated the place. For once, one of Kira's homes was full of color, lots of tasteful art, and comfortable-looking furniture instead of the modern stuff she usually preferred that often made his back hurt just thinking about it. "Where is she?" he asked Lindsey.

"Upstairs, last bedroom on the right."

"Thanks." He nodded to her and then tugged Amelia along with him.

"Do you think I should stay down here while you talk to her?" Amelia asked when they reached the staircase.

"No. This involves all of us. Kira knows you're coming." He gave her a quick kiss on the top of her head. "Don't worry. You belong here with me."

She nodded, but he could tell she was a little bit

uncomfortable. He didn't blame her; so was he. Both of them were about to experience a major privacy invasion if he couldn't figure out how to get them to bury the story.

"Look at those views," Amelia said, staring out the wall of windows on the second-floor bonus room area.

"It's really something. But to be honest, I prefer the redwood valley," Grayson said.

She chuckled. "Seriously? I know it's pretty there, but would you really choose the valley view over this ocean?"

He nodded. "It's where you are."

"Dammit, Grayson. You're going to make me cry again. Do you know how hard it is for a pregnant woman to keep her emotions in check?"

He just chuckled. "You seem to do okay."

Amelia wiped at her eyes and then smiled at him. "You're a little cheesy. Romantic, sure, but cheesy."

He winked. "I try."

When they got to the door at the end of the hall, it was cracked open slightly. Grayson knocked. "Kira?"

"In here," she called.

Grayson pushed the door open and the two of them walked into a room that was completely different from the rest of the house. He'd seen this room before. Only not in person. It was in a vision. There wasn't a glimpse of color anywhere with its white furniture, other than the brilliant blue from the dramatic view of the coastline.

Kira was sprawled on a chaise lounge, wearing a short, white silk robe and nothing else. She held her hand out to him, "Welcome home, Grayson."

He rolled his eyes. "You know this isn't my home and never will be. It's nice though."

She just shrugged one shoulder. "You know my homes are

your homes. It was just an expression." Her voice was tired as if she hadn't gotten much sleep. That wasn't unusual. She barely slept when she was stressed about something. Though he was impressed with how normal she was behaving. At one time, finding out all of her business was going to drop in a magazine article would have sent her spiraling. He wondered what was different this time.

Grayson gestured toward the door where Amelia still stood. "Amelia's here."

Kira immediately sat up and glanced over at her. "Amelia, I'm so sorry you've gotten caught up in this mess. You don't deserve any of this."

"I'm sorry it's happening to you, too," Amelia said, stepping into the room. "It's awful for them to run this story."

Kira turned to Grayson. "You told her everything? The miscarriage and my mom?"

"Not your mom." He grimaced. "I only filled her in on the stuff the reporter asked her for comments on out of respect for your privacy."

Kira gave him a soft smile. "You're a kind man and the best friend I've ever had. But it's too late. The story already leaked online. My lawyers are all over them to post a retraction about the parts that are wrong, but it won't matter now. People will believe what they want to believe."

"It's already leaked?" Grayson asked, pulling his phone out of his pocket. It didn't take long for his eyes to widen in surprise and then narrow in anger.

"It happened about ten minutes ago. I can't apologize enough. Especially to you, Amelia." She rose from her chaise lounge and walked over to her. "I was terrible to you while I was in Keating Hollow. Some of the things I implied were awful. I have no excuse. I guess my only defense is that I was hurting and wanted Grayson to make it all better. Instead, he was focused on you, and I didn't handle it well."

Grayson nearly cried watching Kira apologize to Amelia. The humble woman speaking from her heart was the friend he'd grown up with. The one he'd stood by all these years even when she acted like an entitled actress and appeared to care about no one but herself. He'd known she was still in there. He'd witnessed glimpses of her fairly often, but never in this raw form without any filters or masks.

"I understand, and thank you for the apology. It means a lot," Amelia said, giving her a kind smile.

"You do?" Kira asked, sounding completely taken aback. "But why? I was such a bitch."

Amelia chuckled. "Yeah. You were. But I understand that Grayson is your person, and you see me as a threat to that relationship. It makes sense that in a weak moment you'd lash out."

Grayson moved closer to Amelia and wrapped an arm around her waist. After kissing her temple, he whispered, "You're amazing."

She smiled up at him, her face full of love and understanding. "So are you."

"Ugh. Gag. You two are making me sick," Kira teased. Her eyes were sad, but there was a small smile on her lips.

"Are you going to be okay?" he asked her.

"I will be now that you two are here."

He raised an eyebrow that she pointedly ignored. Grayson was surprised she'd included Amelia in that statement, but he wasn't going to push it. She was trying, and he appreciated it more than she could know. "If you two don't mind, I'm going to step out and see if I can do anything about that story. I don't know how successful I'll be if a giant lawsuit hasn't stopped them, but I can try."

"I'm fine here," Amelia said. Then she glanced at Kira. "If that's okay with you of course. I can go to another room if you want your privacy."

"No. You're welcome here," Kira said and gestured to the couch in the sitting area of her oversized master bedroom. "Take a seat. I'll get you something to drink."

Kira slipped her arm through Grayson's and walked him out of the room into the hallway.

"You're going to get drinks?" he asked her, amused.

"Yes. Me. Is that so impossible to believe?" she asked indignantly.

"No. I've known you since before you were Katy Carmichael, remember? I'm the only one who knows that you can make a mean chocolate cake from scratch and that you always end up overcooking the pasta."

She snorted, and he knew it was because both of those things were true.

Grayson took a moment to really study her before adding, "But look at you. You look like one of those reality TV stars who has staff to handle everything. And to be fair, you usually do these days. What's up with just Lindsey hanging around?"

"I told you. I'm making changes. I just needed some time away from that life, and as incredible as it seems, the simpler things are, the happier I am." She shrugged and then smirked. "It turns out I actually can get my own sparkling water. Who knew?"

"I did." He hugged her and then wondered if he should stop doing that as he glanced at the bedroom where Amelia waited for him. Just as soon as the thought crossed his mind, he dismissed it. She wouldn't want him withholding affection from his best friend because of her. Amelia had a bigger heart than that. When he let Kira go, he said, "Let me see what I can do. Be nice to Amelia, okay?"

"I have been being nice," she said defensively.

"You have. I just want to make sure you keep at it, all right?"

She rolled her eyes. "Yes, Dad." Kira turned and started walking back toward her room.

"Kira?"

"Yeah?"

"It's good to see you. These changes you've made? They're already noticeable."

That tiny smile was back, only this time it actually reached her eyes. "Thanks."

CHAPTER 25

*A*melia stood near the window, staring out at the vast ocean. She wondered what it must be like to have so much money that one could buy a home with such beauty without even batting an eye. Grayson had told her that Katy had multiple homes. It was inconceivable to Amelia, a woman who worked for the firehouse, to comprehend owning even one place like the gorgeous beach house, much less multiples.

"It's gorgeous, isn't it?" Katy said from behind her.

"It's breathtaking. I don't mind admitting that I'm a bit jealous," Amelia said.

Katy let out a huff of laughter. "That makes two of us then."

Amelia turned to eye the actress. She'd managed to change into jeans and a wrap-around shirt that showed off her narrow waist without Amelia noticing. Maybe that was because there was a completely separate dressing room that no doubt had a closet the size of Amelia's house. "Uh, why in the world would you be jealous of me? I work at the firehouse."

Katy's gaze dropped to Amelia's growing belly. Pain flashed over her pretty features before she glanced away.

"Oh, shit." Amelia wished for the floor to open up and swallow her whole. How could she be so careless with her words. "I'm sorry. That was really insensitive of me. I wasn't thinking."

"There's nothing to apologize for," Katy said as she wiped a single tear away. "I know you weren't trying to hurt me."

"I wasn't. Not at all."

Katy didn't respond. She just moved to the couch, curled up in the corner, and covered her legs with a big white fuzzy blanket.

Amelia didn't know what else to say, so she blurted, "That's a really cute top. I like it."

"Thanks. I do, too. Turns out not everything has to be designer in order for it to look good." She made a face, indicating that she was making fun of herself. "Take a seat. If history is any indication, Grayson is going to be a while."

"Sure." Even though she would've preferred to stay where she was and keep studying the dramatic view, she retreated and sat at the other end of the couch.

"There's another blanket here if you need it." Katy pointed to another white throw laying on the back of the couch.

"Thanks. But I'm fine. I'm a fire witch, so I normally run a little warm."

"That must come in handy. I could use that skill," Katy said. "Instead, I'm stuck with a strange spirit talent that seems only to be good for knowing when it's going to snow."

"Really?" Amelia asked, intrigued. "That is strange. Can you tell when it's going to rain?"

"Not unless I look at the weather app. Told ya. It's weird."

"Well, who needs magic when you can act as well as you do, right? That's a far greater talent than most people," Amelia said. "I can't wait for your next movie to come out. It must've been wild working with Maverick Miles. He's gorgeous."

Katy pressed her lips together into a thin line before abruptly changing the subject. "Do you and your mom get along?"

"Um, I guess so," Amelia said. "I wouldn't say we're close, but she loves me, and I love her. She's a good person."

Katy nodded. "If you called her right now, would she pick up the phone?"

"If she was available, sure." Amelia frowned, confused by the line of questioning and the fact that the actress had made a complete U-turn in their conversation. "Kira, I'm sorry. Did I say something wrong when I mentioned Maverick? If so, I didn't mean anything by it. I was just trying to make conversation. I'm not trying to wrangle a meet-and-greet or anything."

She waved an unconcerned hand. "Of course not." Then she chuckled. "It never crossed my mind that you'd be trying to use me to meet more celebrities, so don't worry about that. It's just me. I don't want to talk about acting right now. I'm taking a break, trying to recharge and figure out what I want to do next with my life. Talking about ex… costars just makes that harder. I didn't mean to be rude."

"I see," Amelia said, not missing her pause when she'd said 'ex.' Had she dated Maverick? If so, it made sense that she didn't want to talk about him, but she took the actress at her word that she just didn't want to discuss her job. "Sorry about that. Okay, back to mothers. Do you get along with yours?"

"My adopted mom, yeah. We get along mostly. It's sort of the same. She loves me, and I love her, but we're not super close. She doesn't really get me, and I don't really get her."

"You're adopted?" Amelia said, unable to hide the surprise in her tone. That wasn't something she'd seen coming.

Katy tilted her head to the side. "Grayson didn't tell you?"

Amelia shook her head. "Why would he?"

"The article, it's all in there... oh, wait. He did say he wanted to respect my privacy, didn't he?"

"He did." Amelia agreed. "He's good at that kind of thing."

She let out a sigh and pressed two fingers to her temple, rubbing it. "You're right. He's the best. I'm lucky to have him as a friend."

Amelia opened her mouth to say that she was sure Grayson felt the same way, but Katy started talking again, cutting her off.

"But my birth mom? No. She's not interested in meeting me. Apparently being a successful actress who is offered role after role after role in a business that is more fickle than a tomcat isn't good enough for the great Jeanette Brooks."

Amelia had to force herself not to gasp. Jeanette Brooks? She was like the greatest actress of all time. She'd played every role from Jackie O to Audrey Hepburn and had gotten Oscars for a majority of them. "Wow. That's..."

"Crazy? Insane? Messed up?" Katy said.

"Yeah, all of that," Amelia said. "When did you find out that she's your mother?"

"Not long ago. Less than a month. In fact, it was when I was in Keating Hollow that my lawyer told me she didn't want to meet. I was a complete mess. I'm afraid I took some of it out on you. I'm sorry for that by the way."

"You've already apologized, and it's already forgotten." That was a lie. She'd really caused Amelia a lot of anxiety, but Amelia wasn't going to dwell on it, and she was determined to make friends with Grayson's bestie if it was the last thing she did. She could tell the other woman was hurting, and it was obvious she needed someone to talk to. So despite her instinct not to pry, Amelia asked, "How do you know she doesn't want to meet you? Did you manage to make contact with her?"

"My lawyer spoke to her lawyer. It didn't go well. Now this damned story is out there, and I think Jeanette is going to think I did it on purpose so people would start snooping around and figure out who she is."

"I think I need to read this story," Amelia said. "Because I don't understand why she'd think that."

"Oh, it's printed out over there on the desk." She waved toward an alcove on the other side of the room. "Go on. Read it and then you can tell me if it's as bad as I think it is."

Amelia crossed the room and grabbed the pages. But before she started reading the article, her gaze snagged on a row of photos. One in particular. It was of Grayson standing in a bedroom with a white bed that had furry pink pillows on it. It didn't look anything like the one in the Rhode Island house. But it did look exactly like the one in her vision where she'd seen Katy kiss Grayson. Amelia's heart started to pound against her rib cage, and she felt a little dizzy as she picked up the photo.

"Is that the picture of Grayson at the Cape Cod house?" Katy asked.

"Um, the one with pink pillows on the bed?" Amelia asked, her voice squeaking just a touch.

"Yeah, that one. Doesn't he look really good there? It's my favorite picture of him. He's just so happy."

"Happy," Amelia repeated, starting to go numb. What was she doing there with Katy Carmichael? She'd been really naïve thinking it was a good idea to come there, to try to make friends. They were never going to be friends when Katy had her claws in Amelia's man.

"It's too bad I sold that house. It was really great for parties," Katy said, throwing her head back onto the couch pillow.

"You sold it?" Amelia asked.

"Yeah, right after it went on the market just a few weeks ago. It was wild. Why?"

"No reason," Amelia said, completely confused. Her visions didn't always materialize, but that one had been so clear that she'd been certain it would. But then it hit her. Maybe her vision hadn't been of future events. Maybe it was a memory? That happened sometimes with spirit witches. They just saw things from the past or the future. Not that Amelia was a spirit witch. Her talents were with fire. But since she'd never had a vision before getting pregnant, she assumed they were fueled by the baby, who very well could be a spirit witch just like Grayson.

The tension she hadn't realized she'd been carrying drained right out of her. That meant Grayson wasn't going to leave her for Katy. He hadn't ever intended to, and she'd been right not to trust what she saw. Amelia let out a sigh of relief as she sank into the desk chair.

"What's that sigh about?" Katy asked, eyeing Amelia suspiciously.

"Nothing, I..." Then she decided to just be honest with the actress. What did she have to lose? "It was this vision I had." Amelia described what her mind had shown her and ended with, "So I decided it was just a memory."

Katy's eyes widened. Amelia was fairly certain it wasn't easy to shock the actress, so she took a modicum of pleasure in knowing that she'd succeeded. "You're right. That is a memory.

It's from last December when I called Grayson back to help me bury this very same story."

"What? This same one? How... why... I don't get it," Amelia stammered.

"I know it's nuts. The only new item was about your friend, Victoria. They must've dug that up later. But this group of reporters have been working on this story for a while. Grayson managed to get the magazine that was going to publish it to stand down, but the reporters kept shopping it, and without knowing exactly who they are, we had little chance of stopping it altogether if they found someone else to publish it. So here we are. Back at square one. Or two, maybe, since it was leaked."

So that was why Grayson had left. He'd not only been protecting Katy, he'd been protecting Amelia as well. She didn't love that he'd just disappeared without a trace, but at least she understood it now. And maybe she loved him just a little bit more. "I'd better read this thing."

"I think that's wise." Katy tilted her head back and closed her eyes.

Amelia glanced at the headline: *Star's Turbulent Love Triangle and Secret Shame*.

"Disgusting," she murmured while her stomach churned. What was wrong with people? A whole lot, as it turned out. Because the article was full of half truths about the pregnancy and the D & C. There was a picture of Grayson holding her hand as they left the hospital. And then more lies and sensationalism about Katy's life, including accusations of threesomes and drug addiction. They ended her story by blaming it on the fact that she was adopted and that it was rumored her mother was a famous actress.

Amelia let out a little gasp of horror. No wonder Katy

thought that line might make Jeanette think she was calling her out. The article was horrific, and she hadn't even read about the star's secret lover yet.

Feeling like she needed a shower, she forced herself to continue reading. When she got to the part that was about Grayson, it nearly broke her. The basic facts were correct as far as she could tell, but the author had speculated and psychoanalyzed him through the entire thing, making him sound like a man who was unstable because he'd not only lost his parents when he was young, but he'd also witnessed their deaths.

Amelia gritted her teeth and braced for what they had to say about her. It wasn't much, but it did detail the trauma of losing Victoria and then went on to speculate that Grayson had a thing for broken women. As if witnessing a tragic accident had somehow broken Amelia or that losing a baby had done the same to Katy.

"I hate these people," Amelia said suddenly.

"Join the club." Katy didn't move from her spot on the couch.

Even though she knew better, Amelia took a second to look at the few comments that were visible at the bottom of the page. The first two were typical jerks who were debating Katy's breast size while ignoring the content of the article. But the third one, that one had potential.

I heard from my friend that the actress who is Katy's birth mom is Jeanette Brooks. Pull up pictures of them and you'll see the resemblance. It's in the eyes. And by the way, the only reason they haven't met is because Jeanette doesn't know Katy is looking for her. Her lawyer is her niece, and since Jeanette doesn't have any other kids, the niece is trying to worm her way into being her sole heir.

"Katy! Did you see this?" Amelia called.

"See what?"

"These comments. There's one I think you'll find really interesting."

"All comments are trash. Celebrity lesson number one is never read the comments."

"Too late. I already did." She read the comment out loud and wasn't surprised when Katy popped off the couch and came to read it for herself.

"Holy shit. What if this is true?" Katy said to herself.

"There's a pretty good way to find out." Amelia pulled out her phone and googled Jeanette Brooks' niece. It took all of two seconds to confirm that Jeanette's lawyer really was her niece. "You have to try to make contact with Jeanette again," Amelia insisted. "This smells like a cover-up."

"Smells like a cover-up? Who are you? James Bond?" Katy asked, looking slightly amused.

"You know what I mean. I think this comment might actually be the truth. What can it hurt to try?"

"Everything." Katy pressed a hand to her heart. "It nearly killed me last time. I don't want to go through that again."

Amelia dropped the article back on the desk, and when she saw the look on Katy's face, she felt terrible for even mentioning it. "I'm sorry. I'll drop it."

"Thank you." Katy squeezed her eyes shut and then shook her head as if trying to dislodge thoughts from her mind.

Amelia started to back out of the room to give her privacy, but Katy called, "Wait. Let's see if we can find out any more about this niece."

Forty minutes later, they didn't have anything except an Instagram picture of the niece posing with Silas Ansell. When Amelia saw it, she did a double take but then realized that Silas was doing a movie with Jeanette at that very moment. Likely the niece was a fan and asked for a photo. When Amelia couldn't stop staring at it, Katy got impatient.

"What exactly are you looking at? That IG account is just a wall of celebrity trophy pictures. It's not going to tell you anything."

Amelia tapped Silas's picture and said, "I have an idea."

"What's that?"

"A phone call." Amelia fished Shannon's business card out of her purse and placed it on the table.

CHAPTER 26

It had been one hell of an eventful twenty-four hours. Grayson had spent half a day threatening a dozen people with a lawsuit so large he was certain it would scare them into at least taking down the article. There was no getting rid of it completely, because the internet didn't work that way, but at least the original source would be missing.

No dice.

The online rag didn't seem to care one bit and kept citing the first amendment right to free speech. Grayson was quick to point out that the amendment wouldn't mean one iota in a defamation lawsuit. That also had been ignored, and all of them acted as if they moved through the world without consequences. It was likely they did, but Grayson promised them, and himself, that it wouldn't happen this time. He'd make sure of it.

When Grayson finally got tired of talking to them, he turned to a new plan. All he had to do was convince Kira to go on a national talk show to tell her side before the magazine went to print. It would mean that the first time most people heard her story, it would be from her personally. And the magazine article would suffer a quick death, destined to fade away into oblivion as a sensationalized piece that most people would disregard.

That had gone over like a lead balloon. Or at least it had until Amelia had somehow managed to get a message to Jeanette Brooks that Katy wanted to meet her. And Jeanette had actually been overjoyed. She wanted to know where they could meet and have privacy. Katy had invited her over right that minute, and Jeanette had immediately booked a charter flight from the movie set where she was filming in Canada.

The pair had stayed up all night, talking, sharing acting stories, and crying over their separation. And when Katy broke the news about the article, Jeanette had been the one to insist they tell their story first. With Jeanette on board, they'd quickly booked a segment on *Maven's*, the most popular talk show in the nation.

Now Grayson and Amelia were on the sidelines in the studio in New York, watching as they both tried to set the record straight. Jeanette was the one to go first. She was courageous in talking about her struggle to be a single, barely working actor suddenly having to raise a child and do it while dealing with sexist Hollywood producers. Without any family to help her, Jeanette had felt forced to give her child up for adoption. But she'd waited every day for over thirty years for the call that her child wanted to meet her.

Katy talked about never feeling like she truly fit in with her family, even before she knew she was adopted. And then when she found out, it had all started to make sense. She'd also told the story about how devastated she was when she heard her own mother didn't want to meet her.

Jeanette had reached over to grab Katy's hand, making sure she knew that had never been the case.

The entire hour had been like a free therapy session, but all Grayson cared about was making sure his friend was happy and that he and Amelia could go home.

"I like her," Amelia said.

"Who? Jeanette?"

"Yes, but I meant Jeanette's daughter. Katy Carmichael. She has grit and attitude. It's fun to have a conversation with her… as long as we see eye-to-eye. When we don't? It's kind of a shitshow."

Grayson laughed. "I'm going to have my hands full with both of you for the rest of my life, aren't I?"

Amelia pressed up on her tiptoes, kissed him, and said, "Count on it."

∼

AMELIA AND GRAYSON had been home for all of three days when they decided it was time for Grayson to move into her house permanently. It was foolish for both of them to pay rent when they were always at her house. Getting out of his lease was fairly easy since rental property in Keating Hollow was so scarce. With Wanda's help it hadn't taken long for the property owner to line up a new renter.

It was Friday, and Grayson was looking forward to finally being settled in with Amelia in the house in the hills. Only first, he had to finish packing his stuff. After work, he went straight to his rental, intent on filling his suitcases, but when he walked into his bedroom, he did a double take when he saw the beautiful brunette sprawled over his bed.

Naked.

"It's about time you got home, Grayson," she said in a sultry voice and batted her eyelashes playfully. "I've been waiting."

Grayson raked his eyes over her, licking his lower lip as he envisioned what he wanted to do to her.

"I didn't want you to let go of the rental before your vision came true."

"Huh?" he asked, almost too distracted to process what she'd said. But then it hit him, and he grinned. She'd remembered. The night of Shannon and Brian's wedding, he'd told her he'd had a vision of her naked on his bed. His lips curved into a half smile. "Is this my going away gift or my housewarming gift? I'm not sure."

"Definitely your going away gift," she said. "You'll get your housewarming gift after you're officially moved in."

"Damn, I think I just fell in love with you all over again." He went to work on stripping out of his clothes, eager to be skin to skin with her. Grayson had just had her the night before, but seeing her there like that, offering herself up, was doing things to him that were driving him insane.

Amelia picked up a rose stem that had been lying on the bed and traced her skin from her breast to her hip with the petals.

The slow movement made his mouth water. He was torn between watching her and devouring her. It was no surprise when his desire won out and he crawled over her naked body, ready to lose himself in her.

"I think we might not make it home until sometime tomorrow," she said, tracing his abs with her fingertips.

"Tomorrow? I was thinking sometime on Sunday." He nuzzled her neck and then kissed her skin just over her pulse. "What do you think?"

"Sunday," she breathed as his mouth found more of her.

"Sounds perfect."

Grayson let out a small chuckle and then said, "Amelia?"

"Yeah?"

"I love you."

"I love you, too." Her expression turned soft for a moment before a look of pure joy lit up her face. "Grayson," she said, her eyes filling with tears as she placed a hand over her heart. "Our daughter just sent me a vision. It was beautiful. The three of us together on a picnic down by the river, all of us laughing. She's so gorgeous. Thick blond curls and wide hazel eyes. And the happiest little girl." Her voice hitched as she added, "Our life together with her? You just wait; it's better than either of us can imagine."

Grayson thought his heart was going to burst into a million pieces. This life, with his girls, it was everything he'd always wanted and more. He placed his hand on her belly and said, "Tell me, what do you think about trying for a brother or sister for this precious little one?"

She chuckled. "I think we can make that happen. But we're going to need a lot of practice."

He grinned at her. "Perfect answer."

CHAPTER 27

SIX MONTHS LATER

Georgia Exler sat at the table in Incantation Café staring at her laptop. It was time to start her newest paranormal romance, but as usual, she had no idea where to begin.

Meet cute, she told herself. *Just write a meet cute and the rest will follow.*

Okay, she could do this. All she needed was a charming encounter where two people meet for the first time. What was so hard about that? She'd written dozens of them before. She could certainly do it again. Right?

Wrong.

She actually hadn't been able to write anything at all since she'd moved to Keating Hollow. It wasn't the town's fault. It was her. She was suffering a broken heart, and even though it had been over a year since she'd lost Nick, she still was having trouble writing anything that involved a happily-ever-after.

Maybe she was blocked because she'd been cheated out of hers?

It was possible. But that didn't change the fact that she had deadlines, and if she didn't meet them, paying rent was going to be a bigger problem than making up a meet cute.

She took a deep breath and decided to go back to basics. Write what you know.

Okay, she could do that.

Glancing around the café, she spotted an attractive man, maybe mid to late thirties, with wide shoulders, long legs, and forearms to die for. *What is it about forearms*, she wondered. Most people didn't think forearms were sexy, did they? Well, too bad for them, because they were missing out.

Mr. Forearms over there looked like he wielded an ax like a pro, and she couldn't help imagining him out in the back of her house splitting logs. *Hot.*

The first tingle of an idea niggled at the back of her mind, and Georgia put her fingertips on the keyboard and wrote:

Heather sat in the café, staring at the gorgeous man, wondering if she could tempt him to light her fire. Not the one in the bedroom, though she certainly wasn't opposed to that, not with those forearms. No, she needed someone to help her figure out how to work her new wood-burning stove.

Giggling to herself, she continued to write a funny scene about Heather inviting the man over to help her and him getting the wrong idea, thinking she's looking for an escort.

"What?" Heather exclaimed. "No. Oh. Em. Gee. What do I look like to you? The kind of girl who needs to hire her men?"

He chuckled. "No judgment here, ma'am. Everyone has needs."

Heather glared at him, stalked back to her table and, without breaking eye contact with him, sat in the nearest chair, only to let out a yelp of surprise when she sat on a cake and felt the cool whipped cream frosting seeping through her jeans.

The man she'd apparently propositioned gave her a sexy half grin and said, "I'll see you tomorrow about lighting that fire."

Georgia reread the words she'd written and smiled to herself. It was a decent start that she knew she could build on later, but she'd need a walk in the woods to work out where she was going with it. Understanding that more words weren't going to be useful at that point, Georgia closed the laptop and stored it back into its bag.

"Hey!" Hanna said, coming over to greet her. "You look like you're done working."

"I am for now," Georgia agreed. "How about you? Are you going to come back to the house with me like you'd planned so you can help me with those wisteria vines that are taking over, or do you need to stay here?" Georgia had decided on a whim to move to Keating Hollow when Yvette had casually mentioned needing to find a renter for her house last winter. The previous renter hadn't been much for keeping up the gardens, and Yvette, the good friend that she was, had offered a break on the rent if Georgia wanted to deal with it. Georgia had jumped on it. Today was the day she and Hanna had planned to tackle the vines that had become a small jungle, but the café looked busy, and Georgia wasn't counting on it.

"Sorry. I really do wish I could, but Candy couldn't make it in today due to some test she has to study for, so I'm covering for her. Rain check?"

"Sure." Georgia nodded, knowing her friend didn't have a choice. She understood completely, but she was still sad. She'd been looking forward to the company.

"You know, you could ask Logan," she said, gesturing to Mr. Forearms. "He's new in town and might be willing to help you out. He used to run a nursery before he became a novelist."

Georgia's ears perked up. "He's a novelist? What does he write?"

She shrugged. "Fiction, I think. Fantasy? Science fiction? Something like that."

That was just about perfect. They'd have something in common right away. "Sweet. I think I will." Georgia gave her friend a wink and then walked over to Mr. Forearms.

He glanced up the moment she approached his table. "Oh, good. I'll take another double shot, caramel latte, extra whip."

Georgia just blinked at him for a second. Then, with a shrug, she turned around and went over to the counter where Hanna was already helping another customer. When it was her turn, she ordered his drink.

Hanna laughed when she realized what had happened. And just because she was so tickled, she threw in a piece of cake for Logan as a bonus prize.

"You're a menace. You know that, right?" Georgia said when Hanna couldn't stop giggling.

"Yep." She handed her the drink and the cake and said, "Have fun."

Georgia returned to the table to find it full of notes with a laptop right in the middle, but no Logan. She placed the coffee cup in a rare empty space but didn't have anywhere to put the cake, so she just held it until he came back.

"Oh, thank you. I appreciate it. How much do I owe you?" he asked.

"Nothing. Hanna said it's on the house. Here,"—she handed him the cake—"this too. Something about her being amused that you mistook me for one of the baristas."

He frowned then glanced from her to the counter area and back again. "Huh." He put the cake down and smiled sheepishly up at her. "I must've been so far gone thinking about my next book that I didn't even realize you weren't wearing an apron. I'm so sorry. You really didn't have to get my coffee for me."

She waved a hand, indicating it was no big deal. "It's fine. I'm here practically all the time anyway. I'm probably a barista by default." She waved to her table, where her notebook of ideas was still in plain sight. "I'm a writer, too."

"Really? What do you write?" he asked, his eyes alight with interest.

"Paranormal romance. You?"

"High fantasy." He chuckled as he gestured to his notes. "As you can see, it's getting a little complicated."

She laughed. "I definitely can see that. Are you up for a break to chat with a fellow writer, or are you too busy today?"

"I can take a break," he said, gathering his papers. There were his arms again. Why couldn't she stop staring at his arms?

Logan stopped sorting his papers, and when she finally raised her gaze to his eyes again, *just like that,* she felt that same zing of interest she'd first felt with Nick. It caught her completely off guard and made her take a tiny step back.

"Are you okay... Um, I'm sorry, I didn't catch your name."

"Georgia," she said, her voice a little husky.

"It's nice to meet you, Georgia. I'm Logan." He held out his hand to her. And when she took it and he flashed her a gorgeous smile, that was it. She was a goner. Moon-eyed, heart a-twitter, and she wondered if she'd been transported back to her fifteen-year-old self. Because she was having all the rushes of feelings she hadn't experienced since her freshman year in high school.

"Why don't you have a seat?" he asked.

"Sure," she said, still watching him as she sat down in the chair and felt the squish of cake icing seep through her jeans.

"Oh, hell," Logan said. "I'm so sorry. I forgot I put that there because the table was so messy."

She stared down in complete embarrassment when she

realized what she'd just done, but then she stared open-mouthed at Logan and said, "I can't believe this."

"What? That you sat on my cake?" He shook his head and chuckled softly. "It's just cake. But if you want, I'm more than happy to help you clean it off."

Georgia flushed at his flirting, because she'd like nothing more than to have his hand on her ass at that moment, but then she remembered what she'd been trying to tell him. "No, I can believe I sat on the cake. What I can't believe is that I just wrote a version of this scene right before this happened."

He frowned. "You mean you wrote a scene and then acted it out?"

"No. I just wrote a meet cute, and then a similar version came true with you."

He grinned at her. "You call this a meet cute? You're sitting in cake, Georgia."

"Dammit." Georgia jumped up, scowled at him, and said, "Forget it. Not a meet cute. Just an unfortunate cake situation."

"It's a meet cute," he said with a smirk. "I look forward to bumping into you soon so we see where this new romance goes."

"I just bet you do," she said and then stalked off to do something about the cake. But she made sure to exaggerate the swing of her hips because she knew he was watching. Frosting ass and all.

DEANNA'S BOOK LIST

Witches of Keating Hollow:
Soul of the Witch
Heart of the Witch
Spirit of the Witch
Dreams of the Witch
Courage of the Witch
Love of the Witch
Power of the Witch
Essence of the Witch
Muse of the Witch
Vision of the Witch
Waking of the Witch

Witches of Christmas Grove:
A Witch For Mr. Holiday
A Witch For Mr. Christmas
A Witch For Mr. Winter

Premonition Pointe Novels:
Witching For Grace
Witching For Hope
Witching For Joy
Witching For Clarity
Witching For Moxie
Witching For Kismet

Jade Calhoun Novels:
Haunted on Bourbon Street
Witches of Bourbon Street
Demons of Bourbon Street
Angels of Bourbon Street
Shadows of Bourbon Street
Incubus of Bourbon Street
Bewitched on Bourbon Street
Hexed on Bourbon Street
Dragons of Bourbon Street

Pyper Rayne Novels:
Spirits, Stilettos, and a Silver Bustier
Spirits, Rock Stars, and a Midnight Chocolate Bar
Spirits, Beignets, and a Bayou Biker Gang
Spirits, Diamonds, and a Drive-thru Daiquiri Stand
Spirits, Spells, and Wedding Bells

Ida May Chronicles:
Witched To Death
Witch, Please
Stop Your Witchin'

Crescent City Fae Novels:

Influential Magic
Irresistible Magic
Intoxicating Magic

Last Witch Standing:
Bewitched by Moonlight
Soulless at Sunset
Bloodlust By Midnight
Bitten At Daybreak

Witch Island Brides:
The Wolf's New Year Bride
The Vampire's Last Dance
The Warlock's Enchanted Kiss
The Shifter's First Bite

Destiny Novels:
Defining Destiny
Accepting Fate

Wolves of the Rising Sun:
Jace
Aiden
Luc
Craved
Silas
Darien
Wren

Black Bear Outlaws:
Cyrus
Chase

DEANNA'S BOOK LIST

Cole

Bayou Springs Alien Mail Order Brides:
Zeke
Gunn
Echo

ABOUT THE AUTHOR

New York Times and USA Today bestselling author, Deanna Chase, is a native Californian, transplanted to the slower paced lifestyle of southeastern Louisiana. When she isn't writing, she is often goofing off with her husband in New Orleans or playing with her two shih tzu dogs. For more information and updates on newest releases visit her website at deannachase.com.

Made in the USA
Monee, IL
21 June 2025